WHENEVER YOU ARE NEAR

After her break up from a disastrous engagement, Sienna Churchill is ready to make the most of life again and flies to Spain to work as a travel rep with a friend. However, six months later she returns home to her father's farm — and makes a shocking discovery when a ghost from the past reappears . . .

JEANROSE BUCZYNSKI

WHENEVER YOU ARE NEAR

Complete and Unabridged

LINFORD
Leicester

First published in Great Britain in 2007

First Linford Edition
published 2008

British Library CIP Data

Buczynski, Jeanrose
    Whenever you are near.—Large print ed.—
Linford romance library
    1. Love stories
    2. Large type books
    I. Title
    823.9′2 [F]

    ISBN 978–1–84782–412–7

Published by
F. A. Thorpe (Publishing)
Anstey, Leicestershire

Set by Words & Graphics Ltd.
Anstey, Leicestershire
Printed and bound in Great Britain by
T. J. International Ltd., Padstow, Cornwall

This book is printed on acid-free paper

1

Sienna Churchill stood in the doorway of her fiancé's flat, unable to believe her ears. He obviously hadn't heard her let herself in with her key, and was talking on the phone in the living room.

'Yes, I can,' he said. 'But you'll have to hold off for a while till the wedding at the end of the month. After that, I'll have a lot more control over the farm, I promise, and we can get started.'

There was a pause, and then he went on. 'Oh, don't worry about Sienna. What she doesn't know won't hurt her. She'll do what I tell her after we're married.'

Sienna pushed open the living room door and went in. Nick was sprawled on the sofa with the phone on his chest. He hung up quickly, then got up and came towards her, smiling and holding out his arms.

'This is a nice surprise,' he said, pulling her towards him. 'I wasn't expecting you.'

He smiled his lovely smile, the one that normally made her heart beat a little faster. Not this time.

Sienna moved away from him. 'Obviously,' she said coldly. 'I just overheard you on the phone.'

Nick's smile died quickly. 'I see,' he said slowly. 'What did you hear?'

'Enough to tell me that all the things I've been worrying about are true. And that I don't want to be engaged to you any more.' She slid the small diamond solitaire off her third finger and dropped it into the ashtray on the coffee table. 'And that whatever you were planning with your friend, you can forget. You won't ever be married to me.'

Sienna and Nick had had many arguments over the year that they had known each other. They were usually about money. Nick never seemed to have any, despite buying cars at auction and selling them. Sienna had caught him out in lies too many times and he seemed to evade taxes continually. At first, Nick's soft brown eyes and floppy brown hair, combined with his wide, white smile had always softened her heart, but not this time.

'And as for the farm' she continued, 'What use is it to you even if you did get control over it like you said? It hasn't been farmed for years and there's no chance of planning permission to build on the land. You know that as well as I do. I don't know what you're up to but just forget it.'

She turned and walked out of the flat, and went out to her car. She thought Nick might follow her but he didn't. She knew better than to drive off while she was so angry, and sat for a moment clutching the steering wheel and fuming.

Control of the farm indeed! Control of what? The eighteenth century farmhouse and barns had been in Sienna's mother's family for generations, but hadn't been a working farm for thirty years. Before Sienna's mother had died, five years before, she had begged her husband not to sell the farm and so the remaining family, Sienna and her sister, Abby, and their father still lived on the twenty-acre farm.

They had explored the possibility of building on the land but it was firmly agricultural and well within the green belt, so that would never be a possibility. So what had Nick meant?

Puzzled, Sienna put the key in the ignition and reached out her left hand for the gear stick. The sight of her naked left hand gave her a jolt, and for a minute she felt cut adrift and sad that she was no longer engaged.

Then she remembered how charming Nick Fenwick had been when she met him — how smart and kind and considerate. And how, over the year of their relationship, he had become careless and inconsiderate, and, she believed, not entirely honest in his business dealings.

Deep in her heart, she was glad the relationship was over. It had been too quick — too convenient. Nick had moved into the village from London. He said he wanted to get away from the city. He had seemed different and exciting — renting a flat over the village shop, and travelling back and forth to London to buy and sell cars.

The new man in the village with his good looks and expensive cars had turned many a head and Sienna had felt flattered when he'd singled her out.

Not any more. Impulsively, Sienna pulled out her mobile phone and dialled an old school friend she'd had lunch with the previous week. 'You know you were talking about going to Spain as a travel rep?' she asked after greeting her friend. 'Well, I've changed my mind. I think I'd like to go and train as a rep, too. Can I come over and get the details from you?'

2

It was now six months later and the flight from Spain had been quick, but the taxi ride to the farm from the airport seemed interminable. It was 11 p.m. by the time Sienna approached home. In the back of the taxi, she got her father's letter out of her bag, switched on the passenger light and read it for the hundredth time.

Dear Sienna, it said, *I think it would be better if you came home. Something has happened here which is rather strange, and I need your help and advice. Please come home. Dad.*

Sienna folded the letter and put it back in her bag. The taxi changed gear as it turned down the steep hill to Ashenbourne Farm, and then rumbled over the cattle grid at the entrance. In front of the house she paid the taxi, and noticed a newish white BMW parked on the forecourt. She dismissed it, supposing it to be a friend of Abby's, and let herself in through the ancient front door.

She dropped her bag and stood for a moment, savouring the familiar feel of her home. Nothing had changed as far as she could see. The carved hallstand still stood in the corner, draped with coats and surrounded by Wellingtons and shoes. The beautiful oak staircase still rose gracefully out of the hall. Her grandfather's portrait still hung opposite the front door. But something was missing.

Normally, her father's old sheepdog, Patch, would be pattering across the tiled hall to welcome her. It seemed strange without the normal doggy welcome. From behind the closed door of the living room she could hear a T.V. or a radio, and she went forward eagerly, hoping it was her sister Abby that was home so that they could have a chat about their father before Sienna saw him.

Sienna had always felt a bit guilty about Abby. Their father had never made any secret of his preference for Sienna. Sienna had been his first born, the apple of his eye and had inherited her mother's heavy, straight honey-coloured hair and tall, willowy frame, while Abby, arriving three years later had been a thin, fractious baby with mousy brown hair and no stamina.

Of course, their mother had loved them both equally, and tried to make up for her husband's obvious prefer-ence, but now she was gone, and Sienna sometimes felt that her father should show Abby more attention.

Thinking along these lines, Sienna pushed open the living room door and stopped, unable to believe what she was seeing. Nick was lying in a black leather reclining chair that she hadn't seen before.

As she entered, he reached out, picked up a glass from the table next to him and took a long drink. He dragged his eyes from the T.V. screen and fluttered the fingers of his free hand at Sienna in a wave of greeting.

'Lo, Sienna,' he said lazily. 'Good trip?'

For a moment, Sienna wondered if she was dreaming. She had broken off her relationship with Nick, given him back his ring and made it quite plain that it was over when she went to Spain. And now here he was, lying in her family home watching T.V., looking very comfortable and settled.

'What are you doing here?' she demanded. 'I've told you it's over. How did you know I was arriving tonight anyway?'

'I assure you, darling, I had no idea you were arriving tonight.' Nick took another drink.

'Then what are you doing here? Where's my father? And where is Patch? What's going on here? I want you out now, Nick. If you don't go, I'll have you thrown out! You might as well go. You can't change my mind. There's no chance I'll take you back.'

9

'Why on earth should he want you to take him back?' asked a voice from the doorway and Sienna swung round to face Abby who had come in quietly behind her. 'And why do you always think everything's about you?' she continued. 'It never occurs to you that life goes on even when you run away, does it?'

She looked paler and thinner since Sienna had seen her six months before and there were dark circles under her eyes. Her brown hair was up in a ponytail and it looked thin and wispy. She was dressed any-old-how in jeans and a sweatshirt.

'What on earth are you talking about?' said Sienna. 'I didn't run away. I went to Spain for a change after I finished my relationship with Nick. You knew that.'

'You mean after he dumped you,' said Abby. 'After he got tired of you running up debts on his credit cards and drawing money out of his bank account without his permission? You left him in a really bad state financially and ran away.' She went and sat on the arm of Nick's chair. 'No wonder he dumped you. Not everyone in the world thinks you're wonderful and can do no wrong.'

Sienna winced at Abby's spiteful tone. She wondered why Abby felt so angry about the situation, and why she had believed the lies she'd obviously been told. 'None of that's true, Abby,' she said slowly. 'You know me better than that. We need to have a long talk about this. You've obviously been told some untrue things and we need to set the record straight. But first, Nick's leaving. He's no right to be here.'

Nick sat up in his chair. 'You sure about that?' he asked. 'You see, I want to stay. I like it here. I'm comfortable. What do you think, Abby?'

'I think you should stay.' Abby giggled. 'For once, Sienna isn't going to be calling all the shots. It's about time people realised that I have a say in things around here too! Poor Sienna!

Suddenly she isn't Daddy's little darling and getting all the limelight. It must be so-o-o difficult for her.'

Sienna turned and walked out of the living room. She knew she had to talk to her father and find out what his letter meant, and just what was going on at the farm. She hurried down the flagged passage that led off the hall, and burst into her father's study.

The farmhouse's old adjoining dairy had been converted into an office and a bedroom for Mr Churchill since he had developed heart problems and had difficulty climbing the stairs. Her father was sitting at his desk, hunched over his typewriter, an old Remington that he could not be persuaded to swap for a computer. He laboriously typed all his manuscripts on it, much to the frustration of his publishers. But his books for children had been widely read for over twenty years and had a huge following, so they tolerated it.

Mr Churchill's books brought a good income into the house — more than was needed for the bills and a full-time housekeeper. He looked up in alarm as Sienna burst into his study, and then his face changed and he smiled a smile of pure joy and held out his arms.

'Sienna! Thank God you're home. Oh, I have missed you!'

'I missed you too, Dad. It's lovely to be home.' As Sienna hugged her father, she thought how much more frail he felt than when she'd hugged him before leaving six months before. He'd had his children late in life, he was in his sixties, but seemed somehow older to Sienna. She sat down in the chair next to his and looked into his face.

'Have you managed all right, Dad? I wish I hadn't gone to Spain. It was a mad idea and I was terrible at the job. I've been so worried about you.'

'Don't be silly. You have your own life to lead. You told me exactly why you were going and I didn't blame you. You said you were going away for a complete change after you broke off your engagement, but that Nick . . . '

His face darkened. 'I've heard he's been sort of implying that you ran away because you were ashamed of something you'd done. What rubbish! I told him that you'd gone away after discovering what a crooked so-and-so he was and he's proved that all right, hasn't he?'

'Is that why you wrote to me and asked me to come back?'

'Yes. That and Abby. She seems so different somehow. I need you to find out what's wrong with her. She's so dopey all the time, and hardly speaks to me at all. You know that receptionist job she had at the doctors' surgery? She lost it because she kept having days off without giving a reason. She's like a changed person. I've been so worried. And Patch has disappeared.'

'What? Run away? Surely not. He wouldn't go anywhere without you.'

'I know. That's what is so strange. I had a doctor's appointment and when I got back he'd gone. The doors were all closed but of course he's got his dog flap. He just went. I went all over the farmland calling him but there was no sign. It's just not like him. It's been four days now.'

Sienna took her father's hand. 'Well, I'm back now, Dad, and I'll sort things out, don't you worry. I shouldn't have gone. We've had enough difficulties since Mum died, without me breaking the family up still further. We'll sort things out, don't worry. I'll start looking for a job straight away, I'll find Patch and I'll find out what's wrong with Abby.

'It's probably something really simple, like boyfriend trouble. The first thing I have to do is get Nick out of the house. I don't know who told him I was coming back. I hardly knew myself until last week. I can't think why Abby let him in. She knows we're finished. Why would he come here so late in the evening?'

Mr Churchill turned pale. 'But I assumed you'd spoken to Abby,' he said.

'Yes, just briefly. We couldn't talk

properly because Nick was there. I'll sort things out as soon as I get rid of him, which will be in about five minutes. What a cheek! Coming here. I'll soon sort him out.'

'But Sienna.' Her father had gone paler still. 'I thought she'd told you. He lives here. He and Abby were married two months ago!'

3

Sienna left her father's study, picked up her bag from the hall, and rushed up the stairs to her room. It was exactly as she had left it six months earlier, the bed neatly made up with its patchwork quilt and her old teddy sitting up against the pillow. She felt an overwhelming relief. Everything else seemed to have changed.

The idea of Abby being married was so strange. And to Nick! She wondered how it had come about, and why they had kept it secret from her. A part of her hoped that Abby had fallen in love with Nick and he with her, but the conversation she had overheard all those months ago in Nick's hall filled her with doubt. As she got ready for bed, she felt real fear for Abby.

The ugly things she had said to Sienna a short time before seemed out of character, and the way that she had withheld the news of her marriage while teasing and laughing at Sienna was most unlike the sister that Sienna knew. As she cleaned her teeth at the washbasin in her room, and took off her make-up, Sienna decided that in the morning she would get Abby on her own and sort things out once and for all.

★　★　★

Sienna had been dreaming that she was on the plane again, and something was wrong with the engine. She woke up with a start in pitch darkness, and lay for a moment remembering that she was safe at home in her own bed. And then, very faintly, she heard the heavy engine that had instigated the dream. It seemed to be close by, close enough to wake her anyway.

Quickly, she slipped out of bed, put on her fleece dressing gown and slippers, and went and opened the window. The noise was coming from the old barnyard behind the house. She went quietly out on to the landing, put the light on and crept over to what had always been Abby's bedroom.

The door was ajar and she pushed it open gently and said quietly, 'Abby? Nick? Something's going on behind the house in the barnyard. I heard an engine revving and . . . ' A faint snore came from the double bed and Sienna could see in the strip of brightness from the landing light that only one person was in it.

As she went closer she saw that it was Abby, curled up like a child and sleeping deeply. Of Nick there was no sign.

Sienna took hold of Abby's arm and shook her. Her sister had always been such a light sleeper that Sienna was surprised when she continued to snore, and then on being shaken harder, merely muttered, turned over and slept on.

Puzzled, Sienna continued to shake

her saying, 'Come on, wake up. What's the matter with you?' but all her attempts to wake her sister failed. She was obviously not ill or unconscious, just deeply asleep. Worried, Sienna switched off the landing light and went back to her own room but left the door open on to the landing. She sat cross-legged on her bed and waited.

She was still sitting there, half-an-hour later, when she heard someone come quietly up the stairs. She rushed to her door and switched on the landing light. Nick stood blinking in the sudden brightness. He was wearing a dark sweat suit and moccasins and carrying a glass of milk. He seemed calm and even amused to see Sienna emerge so suddenly from her room.

'Well this is cosy,' he said, smiling. 'Thanks for the offer, but I'm a married man now as you know, so I can't. Sorry and all that.'

For a moment Sienna was lost for words. Then she burst out, 'I'm not waiting here to invite you into my

20

room, you idiot. I want to know why there are vehicles in the barnyard. And what are you doing up at this hour and why won't Abby wake up?'

Nick glanced down at his glass of milk. His voice was patient. 'I'm up at this hour getting this. And Abby's dead tired which is probably why she won't wake up. And as for vehicles in the barnyard, that's probably traffic on the main Ashenbourne Road. You really should curb your imagination, Sienna. You'll be accusing me of being underhanded next. See you in the morning.'

He went into Abby's room and the door closed quietly. Fuming, Sienna went back into her own room and leaned out of the window. All was quiet. A pale moon illuminated the field in front of the house and somewhere in the distance, an owl hooted faintly. She got back into bed, her mind working furiously through what had just happened. Traffic was on the main road? No way. And who gets dressed to

21

go down for a glass of milk?

She asked herself these questions over and over until she fell asleep. This time she dreamed that she was trying to shake Abby awake, but getting no response from her still, cold body. She woke up suddenly in the early hours drenched with cold sweat, and lay, shivering, waiting for the morning.

At seven she was up, dressed and starving hungry. She went quietly downstairs, savouring the familiar sounds of the old farmhouse waking up, and made a full pot of coffee in the machine.

The housekeeper, a sturdy lady called Mrs McKenna, never came in until nine and Sienna knew her father would sleep until she arrived and took his breakfast to him in bed.

As she waited for the coffee to filter through Sienna had a sudden thought and went through the hall and out of the front door. The white BMW was gone so she knew it must be Nick's. Then she went and looked in the garage door and was relieved to see her own

Mini safe and sound where she had left it. She went back into the kitchen, poured two mugs of coffee, and took them upstairs.

In Abby's room she found her sister alone and deep in sleep. Sienna drew back the curtains and went and sat on the bed. Again, it took forever to wake Abby up and when she did open her eyes she seemed not to recognise Sienna. Finally, she sat up, shaking her head and yawning. Sienna handed her the coffee and watched as she drank it.

'You OK?' she asked finally.

Abby shrugged. 'I seem not to be able to get enough sleep lately. I don't know what's wrong with me. I'm fine for days then suddenly I can't wake up. Sorry about last night, Sienna. I was horrible. It was just that Nick said you'd be furious about . . . you know . . . us getting married, and I was sort of expecting a fight. Are you furious?'

'Well, let's say I'm surprised but not furious, no. That would be a bit selfish wouldn't it, since I was the one who broke up with Nick.'

'But he said he broke up with you! He said you'd spent loads of his money and . . . '

'I heard that last night. It isn't true I promise. I went to Spain for a change, that's all. Where is he this morning, by the way?'

'I don't know. I never know. Gone to buy cars I suppose. He doesn't tell me anything.'

'That doesn't matter. The most important thing is — do you love Nick?'

Abby put the mug on the bedside table and lay back on her pillows. 'Yes . . . ' She said uncertainly. 'When he first came around after you'd gone he seemed so lost and lonely and then he was so kind and loving to me I started to fall in love with him and then he proposed. At first I couldn't believe that he could be in love with me after you . . . you always seem to get the best of everything and I get seconds, but he said he'd never really loved you and that he'd kept the relationship going just so's he could see me. But as soon as we were married he seemed to cool off a bit and he isn't half as nice as he was before. I just don't understand.'

Sienna did. She had experienced the same feeling herself soon after their engagement. 'And he's so funny and touchy about his work,' Abby continued. 'He says he buys and sells cars but I never see any. He never seems to have any money.'

'Didn't you ever talk to Dad about it?'

'No. He didn't agree with the wedding. He isn't well and he had a couple of funny turns while you were in Spain. He knows his heart is dicky and he should rest but he says he wants to get on and finish this latest book. I wanted to write to you but Nick said not to. He didn't want you coming back from Spain. And I was so happy when he asked me to marry him. You've always been the most important one in Dad's eyes, and suddenly I felt important. Can you understand?'

'Yes.' said Sienna. 'Yes I can. Please don't worry about it. I'm sure Nick loves you for yourself. Things will work out I'm sure. As long as you and I are all right with each other. I couldn't stand it if we weren't friends. Did you have a lovely wedding? I wish I'd been there.'

Abby rubbed her eyes. 'You didn't miss much. It was a registry office thing. Oh, I wish I could feel a bit more like myself. I'm always so dopey and irritable these days.'

'Have you been to the doctor?'

'Yes. He asked me all the usual questions. Why do doctors always think anyone under twenty-five is on drugs? I told him I might be a bit thick sometimes but I'm not that stupid.'

Both girls laughed and Sienna got up and picked up the mugs. 'But I am worried about Dad,' continued Abby. 'And Patch. Where would he go? I walked the land for hours calling him but he didn't come. He was acting a bit funny for a while, barking in the night and stuff, but nothing too worrying. Where can he be?'

'Let's get some breakfast and things will look better afterwards,' said Sienna. She went downstairs and into the kitchen and started to get toast and eggs ready.

As she went past the key rack on the wall two things happened at once. She noticed that the thick bunch of keys belonging to the barns and outbuildings was missing; and at that moment a heavy duty vehicle rumbled over the cattle grid and into the barnyard.

★ ★ ★

When Sienna arrived, breathless, at the yard, the first thing she saw was that the doors to the small barn were open and a red panel truck was parked in front of them. A tall man in jeans and wellingtons was standing with his back to Sienna, shouting orders into the barn. There was a crash followed by smashing sounds.

'I can't believe you dropped it,' the man said despairingly. 'I told you they were fragile.' Muffled thumps and curses came from the barn and the man clutched his head as if in pain. Sienna strode forwards and stood on tiptoe to tap him on the shoulder. When he swung round she found herself looking into a pair of green eyes set in a face which was scowling horribly.

The man seemed to have fallen into a clay pit. His jeans and T-shirt were plastered and streaked with dried-on pinkish stuff, and even his dark blond hair was spattered. He scowled even more, and said, 'What do you want?'

'I want to know what you're doing putting stuff into this barn.'

'Why do you want to know?'

'Because this is private land and I certainly haven't given you permission to put anything in them?'

The man's tone was angry and he was obviously upset.

Sienna stood up straighter and took a

deep breath. 'I'm Sienna Churchill.'

'Well Sienna Churchill, please go away. I'm busy.'

'I certainly will not. Not until you tell me who you are and what you're doing here!' Sienna's voice was angry, but she was noticing how neatly his dark blond hair was cut, and thinking how handsome his face would be if ever he smiled. She didn't imagine he smiled often. Or spoke until he had something to say.

Unaccountably, she thought of Nick and the way he often gabbled away ten to the dozen whether he had something to say or not. Another crash came from the barn and the man ran inside. Over his shoulder he called, 'Leo. Leo Saville. And I'm putting this stuff in here. Now for Pete's sake leave me alone will you?'

'Not until you tell me who gave you the key.'

'That guy that owns this place. No, don't stack them on top of each other you dope. They're fragile!' Obviously, he was no longer talking to her so she hurried back to the farmhouse.

Abby was up and sitting at the kitchen table. She had finished making the toast and scrambled eggs and had set two places, but Sienna's hunger had disappeared. 'I've just met the rudest man in the barnyard,' she burst out. 'And not only that, he's putting stuff in the little barn. Who said he could do that? Did you? He says the guy who owns the place gave him the key. Was that Dad? Who is he any way?'

Abby laughed and waved her toast at Sienna. 'Was he big and gorgeous with green eyes and a horrible scowl?'

Sienna nodded and Abby continued, 'He was here yesterday talking to Nick. You know, um heap big pow-wow in the living room with no female ears present. Nick must have given him the key.'

'But he had no right! Our family owns the farm, not Nick.'

Abby's expression changed. 'Well I suppose Nick IS family now that he's my husband. Or had you forgotten?'

'Oh no, I hadn't forgotten,' said Sienna bitterly. 'But it still doesn't give him the right if Dad doesn't know.'

'He might have told Dad. There's no need to be so down on him all the time, Sienna. It's like you're always expecting the worst. You're going to have to learn to get along with him you know.'

There was a short silence during which Sienna decided again not to tell Abby about the conversation she had overheard in Nick's hall.

'Stop being so suspicious all the time. Tell me what your plans are now you're back,' continued Abby with her mouth full.

Keep an eye on Nick thought Sienna. Out loud, she said, 'First, find Patch. Dad will be so upset if I don't. I must ring the animal shelter.'

'Oh I did that days ago,' said Abby. 'They haven't got him.'

'Which one? Ashenbourne?'

'Yes. That's where he'd be. He can't have gone far. He can't walk very well. And surely no-one would steal an old dog would they?'

Sienna didn't know. After breakfast, desperate for positive action, she got into the Mini and drove to the animal shelter to check for herself. The staff were very kind and allowed her to look in all the cages. Sienna found it most distressing as all the dogs jumped up eagerly, thinking that their owners had come to take them home, and she was close to tears when she got back into the car.

She sat for a moment and then went back into the shelter's office and asked for the next closest animal shelter. It turned out that it was on the other side of Derby, much too far away for Patch to be in its area, but Sienna was quite desperate by now and asked the receptionist if she would ring the other shelter and ask if they had an old sheepdog in their care. The receptionist held a short conversation on the phone consisting mostly of 'OK' and then hung up the phone and smiled happily at Sienna.

'Old sheepdog. Black and white. Been there for four days. Good luck.'

Later, Sienna did not remember much of the drive through the city and out the other side. She pulled up, spurting gravel in the shelter's car park and rushed inside. The receptionist asked her a few questions, then called an assistant who led her out into the yard where the wire netting runs were.

Patch was lying sadly in his run, his food and water bowls untouched, his muzzle between his paws. The other dogs set up a hopeful barking, but Patch seemed to have given up hope and did not lift his head until Sienna called him. Then he barked a mad, joyous welcome. Sienna knelt down on the concrete and hugged him.

Back in the office she signed some forms, paid a small fee and took official charge of Patch. His collar was missing and he had lost weight. He went happily out to the car and got into the back when Sienna opened the door. She shut him in and went back into the office.

'Can you tell me where he was found and who brought him in?' she asked. 'I'd like to say thank you.' The receptionist consulted a file.

'Found wandering,' she read. 'A Mr Smith brought him in. Sorry, no address or phone number. I do remember a white car though.'

On the drive home Patch seemed to know that he was with one of his family and would soon be back at the farm. As Sienna turned the car into the steep lane down to the farm, he sat up and looked out of the window at the familiar landscape.

Halfway down the lane, Sienna stopped the car to enjoy the sight of the old farmhouse nestled in the hollow. As she did, something caught her eye. Nothing much. Just a flash of silver at head height on a tall bush in the ditch.

Intrigued, she got out of the car and struggled down the ditch's bank, trying to avoid the nettles. When she got close to the bush she cold see that what had caught her eyes was the sun reflecting off a small silver medallion. It was linked to a wide leather strap that was caught by its buckle on a twig. She reached up and unhooked it, then scrambled back up the bank and got into the car.

Then Sienna drove slowly and deliberately down to the farm, a deadly ice-cold hatred gripping her heart. In her mind's eye she saw a car slowing halfway up that track; a lazy arm emerging from the window, casually tossing something out in a smooth arc, expecting it to be lost in the thick undergrowth for ever.

Only a projecting twig had prevented that and given her the first solid, tangible evidence that her suspicions were well founded. It lay on the seat next to her: heartbreakingly, unbelievably but undeniably, Patch's collar.

4

By the time Sienna reached the farmhouse she was quite composed and Patch's collar was firmly fastened around his neck. She noticed that Nick's white BMW was parked in the yard, and smiled as she let herself in through the front door. Patch, delighted to be home, bounded ahead through the kitchen and out to the old dairy, intent only on finding his master. Sienna came into the kitchen a moment later and found Nick and Abby sitting at the table. Nick's face was white, and he was staring after Patch as if he had seen a ghost.

'Hello, you two,' said Sienna cheerfully, sitting down at the table with them. 'Isn't it wonderful? I found Patch. He was a bit farther away than we thought, but he's as right as rain. What's wrong, Nick? You look a bit pale.'

'Nothing's wrong,' Nick mumbled, getting to his feet. 'I have to go out.' It was not his usual, lazy tone. He was visibly unnerved.

'Again?' cried Abby. 'You just came in.'

'So what? I've got things to do. So have you. For one thing, you can start looking for another job. It's not good, sitting around all day like you do.'

Abby looked crestfallen and Sienna opened her mouth to protest but was stopped by a rap on the back door. When she went to open it, she was confronted again by the green-eyed, scowling man from the barn. For a moment they stood and stared at each other.

'Is Nick here?'

'Yes,' said Sienna. Then, remembering his rudeness to her earlier, 'Why?'

'I've brought the key back. He said I had to leave it here, I don't know why. I hope no-one will be disturbing the stuff I've put in the barn.'

Suddenly, Nick was beside her, reaching round her for the key. 'Thanks, Leo.

Don't worry. No-one's going to disturb your stuff. But there's only one key and we can't have it lost. Did you get everything in?'

'Yes.' Leo looked at Sienna. 'Sorry. They had just dropped a box. Didn't upset you, did I?'

Sienna shook her head. 'Oh, no. I'm not that fragile. Can someone tell me what's going on?'

'Nothing's 'going on'. I rented some space, that's all. Didn't Nick tell you?'

'No. Did he tell you he needs Dad's permission before he does anything that concerns the farm?'

'He sort of implied he was the owner.'

'Well, he isn't. My father is. And my father would no more agree to his son-in-law's shady little deals than I would. So why don't you take your . . . stolen property or whatever it is, and get off the farm.'

'See what I have to put up with, Leo?' Nick said. 'She always thinks the worst of me. Don't know why. I'll tell you what. Why don't you walk Miss

Suspicion up to the barn and show her all the silver plate and paintings you've got stashed away?' He handed the key back.

'It would be a pleasure,' said Leo mockingly, and held the door open for Sienna. She swept past him with her head held high and they walked round to the barnyard in an uncomfortable silence until Leo said, 'Look, we seem to have got off on the wrong foot. I don't know why you're so suspicious of Nick and it's none of my business really. I hardly know him. I met him in the village pub, and mentioned I needed storage. He talked as if he owned the farm so I thought it was OK.' They continued to walk side by side and the atmosphere relaxed a little.

'It's rather a long story,' said Sienna. She spoke shortly because she was cross with herself. When she had swept so regally past Leo in the doorway, she'd brushed against him and smelled a mixture of men's cologne, a hint of very fresh, clean sweat, and a very subtle maleness that caught her off guard. It stirred up a feeling in the pit of her stomach that she had never felt before. Not with anyone: certainly not with Nick.

She glanced across at his sturdy forearms and wondered how they would feel around her. Wondered? Too weak a word. Wanted. Definitely.

'So you want me to reveal my all, do you?' asked Leo, breaking into her thoughts.

'I beg your pardon?'

'The stuff in the barn. You want to know what it is?'

Sienna blushed furiously, hoping he hadn't guessed her thoughts. 'Yes, if you don't mind,' she said. 'You see, Dad isn't well and Abby doesn't seem very 'with it' lately and so I feel a bit responsible for the farm.'

They reached the door of the small barn and Leo used the key to let them in. As Sienna went past him again in the narrow doorway, she smelled that elusive scent and shivered slightly.

Leo switched on the light. 'Not very mysterious, really,' he said. He picked a screwdriver up off a nearby box and used it to prise the top off the nearest crate. He rooted around in the straw and withdrew a pottery urn. He held it up on the flat of his hand and Sienna could see that its lines were flawless and its balance perfect.

'Pottery. My own,' continued Leo. 'Made with these two hands on my wheel. Sorry, no silver plate or valuable paintings.' He put the urn back and pressed the lid down.

'It's lovely,' breathed Sienna. 'Are all these crates full of the same thing?'

'Good gracious no. Perish the thought! Each one is different and unique. I sell them in the village to tourists. I exhibit at the annual village fete and I stockpile a few beforehand so's people don't have to wait long when I take orders.' He looked down at his clay-spattered clothes. 'Didn't you know I was a potter? Did you think I was just an extra scruffy bloke?'

'Yes,' said Sienna. 'Extra, extra scruffy.' They both smiled and Sienna trembled inwardly.

She had been right. The smile lit up the green eyes and transformed the scowling face. She glanced up at him and tried to imagine how that firm mouth would feel on her own. Then she realised that she was staring up at him and looked hastily down at the ground. 'We'd better get back,' she said.

Leo locked the barn door behind them. 'Mystery all solved then?' he asked, and Sienna nodded.

'I'm so sorry about that,' she said. 'It's just that Nick . . . doesn't always . . . I mean, sometimes I think . . . sometimes Nick is . . . well, I'm not always sure that what he's doing is . . . ' She broke off, unwilling to voice her fears to a stranger, yet longing to unburden herself to someone.

'People usually sort that sort of thing out before they're married,' said Leo shortly.

'Married? I . . . ' Sienna was interrupted by a shout from the farmhouse. Mrs McKenna was waving and screaming Sienna's name. Both Leo and Sienna broke into a run.

'It's your father,' gabbled the house-keeper as they rushed towards her. 'He just collapsed as we were going into the kitchen. You've got to help him.'

* * *

The scene that greeted them as they hurried into the kitchen was frighten-ing. Mr Churchill was lying on his side on the floor with Abby kneeling beside him. Nick was sitting at the table, his head in his hands. Leo strode forward, lifted Abby effortlessly by her shoulders and put her gently aside. He fell to his knees beside the prone man, listened to his chest and muttered, 'No heartbeat.'

Then he swiftly tipped the older man's head back and pinched his nostrils shut. Leaning down, he covered Mr Churchill's mouth with his own. Finally, he sat up on his knees, linked both his hands and began a rhythmic downward pressure on the chest. 'Get the phone Sienna!' he shouted but she was already dialling 999.

'Ambulance please,' she said in reply to the operator's query. 'It's my father, he fell down and now he's . . . ' She was interrupted by Leo.

'Tell them it's a male, about sixty,' he said. 'I think it's cardiac arrest. I've done CPR and got a heartbeat. We need an ambulance. Tell them someone will be at the end of the lane to direct them.' Sienna repeated what he'd said into the phone. 'Get to the top of the lane, Nick,' continued Leo. 'Show the ambulance where to turn off. I'll stay here in case CPR's needed again.'

'Why me?' said Nick.

'Because you can get there faster than these girls probably. Don't talk about it. JUST GO!'

Nick flinched at the tone, but got up and hurried out through the hall. Abby put her head down on the kitchen table and cried. Leo turned Mr Churchill over onto his side in the recovery position and listened to his heart again. Mrs McKenna bustled in with a blanket and pillow and tried to make Mr Churchill comfortable on the floor. Sienna hung up the phone and went over to where her father lay.

'Is he going to be all right, Leo?' she asked.

'Don't know. Has he had any heart problems before?'

'Yes. Four years ago. Oh I wish I hadn't gone away. This is all my fault!' Suddenly Sienna felt herself gripped by the shoulders and found herself looking up into Leo's face.

'This is NOT your fault, Sienna Churchill,' he said fiercely. 'So stop that right away. Go and get your coat and bag so's Nick can drive you to the hospital.' To Mrs McKenna he said, 'Please go and get any medication Mr Churchill was taking and bring it here. The doctor will need it.'

'I want to go in the ambulance,' said Sienna forlornly.

'Believe me, they won't need you in

the ambulance; they've got enough to do. Get your stuff. Nick will be back to drive you to the hospital in a minute.'

'I won't go anywhere with Nick.'

Leo gave Sienna a strange look and said, 'Well, I'll take you then. Get your stuff.'

It took Sienna exactly eleven minutes to get ready to go, by which time the ambulance men were in the kitchen. They wrapped Mr Churchill in blankets, strapped him onto a trolley and were gone in minutes. Nick came panting back into the kitchen and got a beer out of the fridge. Abby looked pointedly at her watch.

'It's going to be a long day, Nick,' said Leo. 'Probably better to lay off the booze for now.'

Nick tipped the bottle and drank deeply. 'When I want advice on life from a potter, I'll let you know,' he said nastily. 'Can I have the keys back?'

'Yes.' Leo passed them over. 'But I'd better drive Sienna and her sister to the hospital at Derby. You two ready?'

'Abby's not going anywhere,' said Nick. 'Ring us when you have news on the old man. We'll stay here and mind the fort.'

Leo looked at Nick for a long time. 'Sienna needs your help,' he said.

'Oh Sienna will manage all right without me, I assure you,' said Nick. 'She's a big strong girl with a mind of her own. Best let her get on with it.'

Sienna gave Nick a withering look. He seemed thin and gangly next to Leo, and his floppy brown hair looked almost feminine compared to the other man's neat head. 'He's right, Leo,' she said. 'I don't need Nick. He doesn't care about me.'

'Then he's a fool,' said Leo harshly, and ushered Sienna out of the door.

* * *

When they got to the hospital it took some time to find out where Mr Churchill had been taken. Sienna's legs felt weak and she found she was trembling. As they walked up an endless corridor, she found Leo's arm around her, supporting her, and warming her back in a most comforting way. It was a small thing, but in this time of stress she found herself immensely grateful for it.

In the end, he found her a seat and went off to find out where Mr Churchill had been taken. He fetched her finally and she was shown into a small office where a very young doctor broke the news of her father's second heart attack in the ambulance, and the fact that he had not survived it.

Sienna found herself numb and unable to speak. It was Leo who picked up her bag and led her out into the bleak corridor, and Leo who walked her out into the hospital car park and towards the car. How Sienna found herself in his arms she had no idea. She only knew that the feel of his warm, solid body against hers was the most comforting thing on earth and his strong hand firmly stroking her hair made everything bearable.

Leo pushed her away reluctantly. 'Sorry,' he said huskily. 'I've got no right to do this. I'd better get you home. 'You can sort out the details tomorrow; you've had enough for one day. Perhaps that husband of yours can come down here and do the paper-work.'

'Husband?'

'Nick.'

'Nick's married to Abby, Leo. She's my sister.'

'Thank God for that,' said Leo, and opened the car door for her. She wanted to ask him what he meant, but suddenly the fact of her father's death hit her like a sledgehammer and she dropped down into the car seat and hid her face in her hands.

'Easy now,' said Leo. 'Just take a deep breath and lean on me.'

Some time later he started the car and drove carefully out of the hospital. His car was an automatic, and so he drove with Sienna still clutching his hand. Halfway home she sat up and let go of it.

Something inside her told her that she must get home and be strong for Abby. No matter what happened now, things at Ashenbourne Farm would never be the same again.

5

A week later, Sienna, Nick and Abby sat in the living room after dinner, drinking coffee. Nick had made it, and brought Abby's cup to where she sat. He was being extremely kind and attentive to her — a far cry from his normal behaviour. It made Sienna feel sick. Since the news of Mr Churchill's death had reached Nick, he had completely changed towards Abby and Sienna suspected that she knew why. The funeral was to be the following day, and the will was to be read the day after that. She gritted her teeth as Nick pushed the footstool up for Abby and asked her if the coffee was all right.

'Yes thanks, Nick,' replied Abby gratefully. 'You are good to me.' She seemed a bit more alert than when Sienna first came home and was enjoying the unusual attention from Nick.

Patch lay in his basket in the kitchen, obviously missing his owner. Over the previous week both Sienna and Abby had tried to persuade him to eat, but he had just picked at his food and lain sadly down again. Nick had been impatient. 'It's just a dog!' he'd said crossly to Abby when she'd cried over Patch's distress. 'Don't be silly.'

The sound of a car outside brought Sienna to her feet. 'You expecting anyone, Nick?' she asked.

Nick shook his head, so she went out into the hall. It was a fine evening and the door was standing open. There was no-one in sight so Sienna stepped outside.

Leo was standing on the gravel drive. His clay-spattered clothes had been swapped for a white polo shirt and chinos. It didn't make that much difference. He was still very tall and rather handsome and the green eyes were just as bright.

In the week since he'd taken Sienna to the hospital, she'd been so busy and distracted trying to organise the house and make sure that Abby was all right, that she had pushed him to the back of her mind. Or tried to.

'Hello,' she said, feeling vaguely happy for the first time since her father's death. 'I'm so glad you've come. I wanted to thank you for your help on the day my . . . when we went to the hospital. You were so kind.'

Leo smiled his transforming smile. 'No thanks needed,' he said gently. 'Are you and Abby OK?'

'We're coping, thanks. At least we're doing better than poor Patch. He's stopped eating.'

'I wondered about that,' said Leo. He gave a shrill whistle and a young black and white spaniel emerged from the shrubbery, rushed up to him and sat down. 'This is Max,' he continued, fondling the dog's ears. 'He's mine. I brought him over because sometimes when old dogs lose their owners they go into depression and it occurred to me that Max might help if that was the case.'

'Patch certainly isn't himself,' said Sienna. 'Please come in, Leo. It's lovely to see you.' As she took him past the living room, Abby waved a friendly hello, but Nick hardly looked up from his newspaper. In the kitchen Leo leaned against the table and watched the two dogs.

At first Patch did not acknowledge the little spaniel, but the younger dog was determined to play. Eventually, it took Patch's squeaky bone from out of his basket and ran around the kitchen with it. Unable to tolerate such cheek, Patch ambled out of his basket and went to give the scamp a telling off. But it developed into a friendly tug of war, accompanied by loud squeaking sounds from the toy.

Sienna and Leo couldn't help but laugh at their antics. Finally both dogs stopped at the water bowl for a drink, and from there Patch noticed his full food bowl, decided he was hungry, and tucked in.

'You seem to know how to handle

most situations,' said Sienna. 'Will you bring Max again? I'd love to see you — both.'

Leo reached out his arm and drew Sienna to him. Then he bent and kissed the top of her head. It was the gentlest, friendliest gesture that any man had ever made and Sienna felt bereft when he let her go and moved away. She wanted more, and she didn't care if it was gentle or not. She wanted to feel his strength and his body warmth against her own body again.

'Will you be at the funeral tomorrow?' she called after him. 'It's two-thirty at St Giles.'

'Of course I'll be there,' he said over his shoulder, and was gone. Sienna went back into the living room.

'What did he want?' asked Nick grumpily. Sienna explained the reason for his visit and Abby rushed off into the kitchen to see that Patch was really eating.

Nick cleared his throat. 'There's something I've been wanting to say to you, Sienna,' he began. When Sienna didn't answer, he went on, 'About the farm. Now that your father's dead, the farm will belong to you and Abby. I'm Abby's husband so I share her half.'

'So?'

'Let's not have any more of this bossy, bossy attitude of yours about what happens here at the farm, eh? You just mind your own business and don't bother me with what you think I should or shouldn't do. OK?'

Sienna was speechless for a moment but soon found her voice. Suddenly she felt ready to say what she wanted to say all along and it came tumbling out in a torrent. 'Oh, don't worry, Nick. I don't suppose what I think or do will make any difference to your shady little deals. I know that you aren't honest and I know that you're planning something but I don't care. All I care about is Abby, and let me tell you this. I don't know how you persuaded her to marry you, but I know you aren't in love with her or even care about her. You're a shabby little conman out for himself and nobody else and if you hurt her in any way, you'll have me to deal with and I can be very difficult where my family is concerned. Do you understand?'

'Understand what?' said Abby, coming back into the room.

'Sienna just wants it to be plain that she's got over her feelings for me and from now on, as we are going to own half-shares of the farm, that we all should get on a bit better and stop being so suspicious all the time.'

'How lovely,' said Abby. 'Do you mean it, Sienna? No more of that awful tension? And you are silly, Nick. Sienna's been over you for ages.'

Sienna got up to go upstairs to her room. As she left, Nick said softly to Abby, 'Come and sit on the sofa with me. I'll give you a neck rub. Now we're home owners we ought to make plans for the future.'

★ ★ ★

Sienna woke up on the morning of her father's funeral feeling very strange indeed. Despite having slept for eight hours she felt tired and unready for the day. A dull headache pulsed away behind her eyes. Showering and getting into a dark dress seemed like an enormous task and she was grateful when she was finally ready to go downstairs. In the kitchen she was surprised to find Abby dressed much as she was, but Nick in a T-shirt and faded jeans, reading the paper.

'Thanks, Nick,' she said as she poured coffee for herself. 'My father would have appreciated you making such an effort at his funeral.'

'Not going,' Nick said without looking up.

Sienna glanced at Abby who was keeping her eyes downcast. 'Well, did it occur to you that Abby might need a bit of support,' she said bitterly.

'Abby will be OK. She doesn't need me fussing and holding her hand. Do you, babe?'

'I suppose not,' said Abby quietly. She got up and put her dishes in the sink. 'Are we keeping Mrs McKenna on by the way? Do we need her now that Dad . . . not that . . . now . . . ' She gulped gave up, and busied herself with the dishes.

'I don't know,' said Sienna truthfully. 'I'm not even sure how much money Dad had. He always dealt with finance. I mean, there's Mum's money too, that her parents left her. That must be somewhere. I'll be able to give you a much better answer after the will's been read this afternoon and I find out what Dad planned for us both.' She turned to Nick. 'I suppose you're coming to that?'

'Of course I'll be there,' said Nick shortly.

The echo of Leo's words, spoken in such a different tone and having such a different meaning hit Sienna like a blow. Suddenly she wanted more than anything to feel Leo close to her. She knew it was silly, but he seemed to give her strength just by his presence.

'I'll drive us, Abby,' she said. 'Better get ready.'

★ ★ ★

At the church she found herself unable to keep from staring round, looking for Leo's neat, cropped head in the crowd. When she saw him, sitting at the back wearing a dark suit and a very white shirt, she let her breath out suddenly and audibly.

The service was very short, as per her father's wishes. He had specifically requested that neither of his daughters be asked to speak, and both girls were very glad of that.

At the graveside Sienna held Abby's hand and tried to comfort her as much as possible. Sienna sensed, rather than saw, Leo arrive behind them. He put a strong arm around each girl and held them to him during the short ceremony. Abby cried softly against Leo's jacket; Sienna was confused by a wholly inappropriate desire to reach up and pull Leo's head down to her own and finally lose herself in a kiss.

She felt ashamed by this wanton desire at her own father's funeral and tried to move away a little, but Leo wasn't having any and kept a firm arm around both the girls' shoulders.

Afterwards, he walked them to the car park with a group of neighbours from a nearby farm, Sienna was loathe to let him go so soon. He seemed to pop in and out of her life, each time leaving her more mixed up.

'Do you need a lift, Leo?' she asked, trying to keep her voice light.

'No thanks, I'm being picked up.' His eyes scanned the car park. At one end a small silver sports car shot into view and accelerated towards them. The top was down and Sienna could see that it was driven by a very attractive woman with her bleached white hair cut in a short crop.

She pulled up alongside them and pushed open the door. Leo folded his long frame into the car and looked back at Sienna. 'Take care of Abby,' he mouthed, and then the car shot off.

Sienna stood quite still. Next to her, a neighbour said casually to her friend as they moved off, 'I haven't seen Leo's wife for ages.'

A flock of rooks flew up from a nearby tree, cawing dementedly. A thin drizzle had begun to fall. And now the awful task of listening to her father's will. Suddenly the world seemed like a very dismal place indeed. Her father was dead. Abby was married to Nick. And Leo had a wife.

★ ★ ★

At the solicitor's office it wasn't much better. Nick was waiting for them, freshly shaved and now in a suit. He greeted Abby warmly and kissed her. He was at his best today, ushering Abby into the solicitor's office and finding her a chair. Sienna wondered how he kept from rubbing his hands together. She sat down numbly and waited.

It didn't take long. Mr Churchill had left his entire estate, consisting of the farmhouse, three hundred thousand pounds and the royalties to his books, to Sienna. Nick leaped to his feet and his chair fell over backwards. His face was deathly pale. 'All to Sienna?' he shouted. 'All? What sort of a father is he?'

But it made no difference. Except for a sealed letter addressed to Sienna, that was the extent of the will. Nick left with Abby, talking loudly about contesting the will. When the door closed behind them, Sienna opened her father's letter. It seemed strange to be reading a second letter from him within two weeks, and each time under such different circumstances.

My dear Sienna, it read. *Because you're a very clever girl you will know why I have not left anything to Abby. I am sure that Nick (or someone very like him) would relieve her of any money or* property which she came into. We have never spoken of it, but Abby is not equipped to deal with the modern world. That is why I am asking you to take care of her.

Let her live at the farm, and please arrange an allowance for her which will enable her to live comfortably. You will be surprised to learn that Abby and I have spoken of these things and she confessed that she would be uncomfortable having control of any finances or property. So she will not be judging me too harshly.

Ask her to look after Patch if he is alive when you read this. To you, my darling daughter, I wish you a happy life and someone wonderful with whom to share it. Love. Dad.

It was dated on the day of Abby's wedding.

The wise, measured tone of her father's letter brought the memory of him too close. Sienna thanked the solicitor and stumbled down the stairs and into the street. She was going to have to be very strong indeed over the next few days. Tolerate Nick's fury. Look after Abby. Take control of the farmhouse and its finances.

And Leo had a wife.

6

The following day, Sienna was up at eight. She donned her blue-denim bib overalls over a white cotton shirt, tied her heavy honey-coloured hair back in a knot, and came downstairs determined to get on with her life. If Leo had a wife then that was the end of that little dream and she might as well admit it.

Nick was at the table, reading the paper and drinking tea. He was still in pyjama bottoms and a T-shirt. His hair looked greasy and needed a wash. Sienna wondered how she had ever had any sort of feelings for him, and experienced a surge of anger when she thought how he had manipulated Abby. Thank goodness her father had done what he had done. The idea of part-owning a house with Nick was unthinkable!

Nick looked up from his paper.

'Before you say anything, Sienna, I'll just say that if you've got any grand ideas about showing me the door, just remember that if I go, Abby goes too. And if I go, I might just move to . . . oh, I don't know . . . France or Spain or somewhere nice and hot. And you won't be able to keep a sisterly eye on our little girl then, will you?'

Sienna stopped filling the coffee machine and looked directly at Nick. 'You are a silly little man,' she said levelly. 'You can't speak Spanish or French and so you certainly couldn't work there. And if you leave here you'll have to rent a house for the two of you and buy food for you both. Oh dear. Marriage does have its downside doesn't it? And you won't leave Abby. You married her for some reason and I'll look forward to finding out what that is. In the meantime, I want all the keys to the barns, and I want them now.'

Nick had looked a little crestfallen when his threats had failed to intimidate Sienna. Now he perked up a little and smiled. 'Sorry,' he said. 'I seem to have mislaid them. Perhaps they are at my old flat. Yes, yes,' he continued, seeing her look of surprise. 'I still have it. And that is where the keys will stay until I decide to give them to you. So quit being so bossy.'

He got up and came around the table towards Sienna. His tone changed. 'C'mon,' he said softly, reaching for her. 'You used to like it when I kissed you. How about a little one now for old time's sake?'

'Ugh. Aren't you horrible? Get off me for goodness sake.' Sienna was retreating round the table, slapping Nick's hands away from her. He cornered her against the Aga and pressed himself up against her. His lips crushed down on hers despite her squirming and fighting.

How long the kiss would have gone on Sienna didn't know, but at that moment the kitchen door opened and Abby's voice asked plaintively, 'What's going on?'

Nick leapt backwards away from

Sienna and burst out, 'I said no, Sienna. I'm sorry but I'm married to Abby now and you can't do this!' He came across to where Abby was standing, white-faced and put his arm around her small frame. 'Sorry babe, but Sienna forgets sometimes that we aren't engaged any more.'

Abby's face crumpled. 'Oh Sienna. You said that was all over! You lied to me! And here you are trying to kiss Nick while you thought I was upstairs. You don't care about me at all you rotten thing. You just care about yourself!'

There was a knock on the open back door and suddenly Leo was there. He looked from Sienna's furious face to Nick's triumphant one and then to Abby's stricken one. 'I think I've come at a bad time,' he said slowly. 'I'll come back.' He was backing out of the door when Abby rushed over to him.

'You did arrive at a bad time, Leo,' she said. 'I just came downstairs and found Sienna all over Nick. It isn't over at all like she said. She's still in love with him. Aren't you Sienna?'

'Still?'

'Yes. They were engaged before Nick and I were married. And she still loves him.'

Leo turned to Sienna. 'Want to go for a walk?' He said quietly, took her arm, and walked her out of the door, shutting it behind them. Like before, they walked in silence to the barnyard, and Leo sat on the low stone wall. 'Right Sienna,' he said. 'I find it hard to believe that you were engaged to that fellow but if Abby says so it must be. But throwing yourself at him after he married Abby? That doesn't sound like you.'

Suddenly, the strain of the last week was too much for Sienna. She felt her legs turn to jelly, and hastily sat down on the wall next to Leo. He steadied her and she leaned against him as she had been dying to do for so long and it all came tumbling out.

'Of course I didn't make a pass at

Nick. He's horrible and I can't believe I was once engaged to him. And now he's married Abby for some reason and I can't work out what it is because he doesn't love her one bit and I think he tried to get rid of Patch, and he's got the keys to the barns and won't give them back and Dad left Abby in my care and if I don't give Nick his way he'll move somewhere else and she'll go with him because she loves him, and I've got to sort out the farm's finances and decide whether to keep the housekeeper on and Dad is dead and you . . . ' She nearly said, 'are married' but changed it to, 'Must think me an awful fool.'

'No Sienna Churchill. Not a fool.' And he kissed her.

It was the kind of kiss that Sienna had dreamed about; the sort that said, 'Forget everything else and think about me.' The pent-up jumble of the past week's troubles seemed to melt into the background and left her feeling totally involved in Leo's nearness and warmth.

She wanted to sink into it like quicksand: to lose herself entirely and forget about the farmhouse and its troubles.

After a while, Leo lifted his head. 'Better?' he said, and Sienna nodded. 'Good,' he said. 'Now. You're bright and clever and you'll sort the finances in time. I wouldn't worry about Nick taking Abby anywhere. He'd have to find somewhere to live and support them both and I'd like to bet that isn't on his agenda. And why not keep the housekeeper on till you've sorted things out a bit more? Then decide. With regards to the barns, I'll get the keys from Nick if you want and you can open them up and see what he's up to.'

If only it was that simple thought Sienna. If only a man came into your life, gave you his strength, treated you like a dear friend, kissed you gently but tenderly, and offered to sort out the worst problems you'd ever had. But the memory of the woman in the red sports car came crowding back, and the neighbour's words echoed in her head.

'Thanks Leo,' she said softly. 'That would be wonderful. But I think it would be better if we kept our friendship platonic don't you? I mean, it would be better if you didn't . . . er . . . kiss me again or anything.'

She stood up. 'Let's go back to the house and make things right with Abby shall we? Oh, I forgot to ask you why you came round today?'

'Oh, I brought Max round to see Patch and perk him up a bit. He's in the car. And . . . well, I wanted to see you, Sienna. There was something I wanted to say but you've made it plain that you'd rather I didn't, so I'll just get Max out of the car and take both dogs for a walk if you don't mind.'

As they walked back up to the farmhouse together, Sienna was thinking how some men, however nice, seemed to cheat and lie. She tried to imagine having a husband like Leo, and finding out that he was kissing other women as he had kissed her. It was an intolerable thought and she stopped dead in her tracks and turned to him.

'I might as well say this Leo despite you being so kind to me. I'm not really impressed with men who are married and who go around kissing other women. It just ends up hurting everyone. If I had a husband like you and I found out that he'd been kissing someone else well, I don't think I could bear it.'

'You mean I can only kiss you if I get unmarried?' Leo said, smiling. 'No problem.' And he kissed her again. When it ended he said, 'That was my ex-wife in the car. We married when we were both eighteen, much too young. We've stayed good friends, although I haven't seen her for a few years. She and her husband are here visiting and they came and bought some pottery. They are staying with friends of mine and she offered to pick me up from the church as my car was in the shop.'

A great surge of joy made Sienna tremble. 'Not married?' she whispered.

'Nope. Free as a bird. And wanting very much to get to know you. So please let me help you sort Nick out and get things back on track. And when they are perhaps we'll have time to think about us.'

Suddenly, the world seemed to swing back on its axis. As they continued back to the house Sienna felt strong and capable of handling almost anything. They separated at the house; Leo went to get his dog and Sienna went to find Abby. She found her alone in the sitting room, staring blankly at the TV.

'You needn't bother saying sorry, Sienna. It's no good. Nick says you've been after him since you got home and just won't leave him alone. It's not fair! He's my husband. Get one of your own! I wish Dad was here. He'd tell me what to do. You just stay away from Nick, that's all. He doesn't want you, he wants me. You say you love me but you don't if you go after my husband.' Abby was gone, slamming the door after her.

Sienna sat down miserably in the armchair. She wished that Leo would come back. She felt mean and deceitful, as if she really had been chasing after her sister's husband.

She felt physically uncomfortable too. Something was sticking into the back of her leg. She got up quickly and looked down at what she'd been sitting on. It was a single Yale key on a cheap chrome ring.

She recognised it immediately. She'd seen it on the hall table, next to Nick's car keys many times. Nick's key. But to what? Quickly, she slid it into her pocket. As she went to look for Leo and the dogs, she told herself that in love and war all things are fair. If the key in her pocket was, as she suspected, the key to his old flat, then like in all wars, there was some spying to be done.

★   ★   ★

Dinner that night was a miserable affair, despite the delicious lamb casserole that

76

the housekeeper had left for them. Abby wouldn't even look at Sienna and kept her eyes on her plate. Nick seemed tremendously pleased with himself and cast sly glances across the table at Sienna. Sienna toyed with the food on her plate miserably, wishing that she could make Abby believe her.

Halfway through dinner the phone rang and Nick went out into the hall to answer it. When he came back his face was like thunder and he sat down without a word and continued his meal.

'Trouble?' asked Sienna innocently.

'It was that Leo bloke. I don't know who he thinks he is. He wants to look in the barns. He's coming around here in the morning and he says if I won't give him the keys he'll bring a policeman friend of his around and make me. I suppose this is all your doing, Sienna? He wouldn't be calling in the police unless he had the owner's support. Well, let the interfering oaf do his worst. He can look all he wants. He won't find anything.'

'I thought the barn keys were at your old flat,' said Sienna.

Nick smiled. 'Oh, I forgot. Woops. I had them here all the time.'

'Why have you still got your old flat?' Abby asked, puzzled. Sienna breathed a sigh of relief. She didn't want Nick going to his old flat and discovering the loss of his flat key just yet.

'I need a place to keep my files, babe, to save cluttering this house up.'

Abby seemed content with this answer but Sienna gazed around the vast kitchen of the enormous farmhouse and thought Liar! Liar! Liar!

After dinner Nick made the coffee as usual. Nick and Abby took theirs into the lounge but Sienna stayed in the kitchen.

Things did seem to be sorting themselves out a bit. Mrs McKenna had agreed to stay on at her normal wage and take care of the shopping, cooking and cleaning. Nick was going to be forced to open up the barns and show what he was hiding.

If Sienna could only make things right with Abby, then the world would seem a much brighter place. But to do so she would have to tell her the truth about Nick, break her heart and risk alienating her forever; an impossible decision.

Eventually, worn out with the constant worry of the situation, she went to bed early and was soon tucked up under her old patchwork quilt. Once again, the thought of Leo was foremost in her thoughts. She couldn't help remember the kiss, and his calm assurances that everything would work out eventually. When the phone by her bed rang she was quite irritated to be dragged away from her thoughts of him, but the sound of his mellow voice on the phone filled her with happiness.

'Sienna? It's Leo. Sorry it's so late. I'll be there about ten in the morning, I've told Nick he has to open the barns. Can you be there?'

'Yes, of course. Thank you for ringing. I'll see you in the morning then.'

The sound of his voice had stirred emotions she'd been trying to keep buried. Sure that she wouldn't sleep, Sienna fetched a book from her shelf and lay down to read. But the words kept blurring and her eyes kept closing and soon the book fell from her hand.

Once again in her dream the plane was diving and the pilot was revving the engine but this time Patch was on the plane with her and his constant barking was driving everyone mad. When she half woke up she realised that Patch really was barking, but far away in the farmhouse, behind a closed door.

She wanted to go and see where he was shut in but the effort of lifting her head from the pillow was too much and her eyes seemed glued together. Soon she was fast asleep again, but the rumble of distant vehicles continued, and Patch barked on, unheard.

7

Patch had been locked in the old dairy all night. Someone had moved the old stone jar that always held the door propped open and let it close to. Patch was distraught and urgently needing to go out when Sienna discovered him the following morning. Her fury at finding him purposely locked in, combined with the dull headache she'd woken up with, did nothing to improve her spirits, and she was dull and lethargic when she answered the door to Leo at ten. He looked closely at her for a moment, then asked gently, 'Bad night?'

'Awful,' agreed Sienna. 'I was having a terrible dream and Patch was barking and . . . oh, I don't want to bore you with this.'

'Yes. Bore me with it. Go on.'

'And then I fell asleep and when I tried to wake up I couldn't. And I could hear Patch barking but couldn't be bothered to get up and look if he was all right which is most unlike me, and well, I felt rotten when I finally did wake up.'

Leo reached out and took hold of Sienna's chin. He lowered his face to hers but only looked intently into her eyes. 'Hmmmmm.' He said. 'Let's find Nick shall we?'

Nick was sitting on the wall outside the back door. He looked spruce and pleased with himself and Sienna's heart sank. He didn't look like someone who was going to have to reveal his guilty little secret; he looked like a man who was positively enjoying himself.

'All ready are we?' he said, jumping off the wall. 'Brought the entire Derbyshire Constabulary with you have you, Leo? Good. Let's get on shall we then?'

★ ★ ★

There was nothing in the barns. The doors stood wide open and the sunshine

82

flooded on to the flagged floors. The huge metal sliding door of the biggest barn was pushed to one side and it was plain to see that nothing was hidden inside.

Nick was beside himself. He kept picking bits of old hay off the floor, pretending to look under them and shouting, 'Nothing here!' In the end he called a cheery goodbye and was leaving when Leo caught him roughly by the shoulder and swung him round.

'I don't see the keys,' he said. 'I'd like them before you go.'

Nick snatched his shoulder back. 'Oh do you want the keys as well?' he asked, sounding surprised. 'I thought you just wanted to look in the barns. Sorry feller, I seem to have mislaid them. I'll come back and lock up sometime when I feel like it. In the meantime . . . ' He glanced around the empty barns. 'Not much that can be stolen is there?' And he was gone, walking jauntily back up to the house, whistling.

'Whatever was in here, went out last

night,' said Leo thoughtfully. He dropped to one knee and rubbed the flagstone with his finger. 'It's my fault for giving him notice. Something was leaking oil here very recently. I think we need to find out what, don't you?'

They went back to the house and discovered that both Abby and Nick had gone. Sienna made coffee and they took their mugs outside and sat on a bench by the back door in the sun.

'Listen carefully to me, Sienna because this is important,' Leo said. 'I don't know what Nick's up to but I don't like it. Tell me, does he ever pour drinks at night for you?'

'No,' said Sienna. 'He sometimes has wine but Abby and I don't drink much at all. Except coffee. After dinner.'

'Who makes that?'

'Nick usually. Oh Leo, you don't think . . . '

'I don't know what I think. But for now you do without after-dinner coffee made by Nick. All right? I'm off now, but I'll be in touch.'

He went without giving Sienna a kiss or a hug, and she felt totally alone when he had gone. She wandered into the kitchen and found Mrs McKenna loading the dishwasher. She told Sienna that Nick had taken Abby to London for the day.

From that moment on Sienna knew what she was going to do. She thought about it while she walked Patch across the field, trying to persuade herself that such a sneaky thing was not within her power, that she should abandon the idea, that it was dangerous and foolhardy. But in her heart she knew that these arguments held no weight and at noon she was heading down the road to Ashenbourne.

Nick's flat was over the village shop. It was accessed via a narrow passage down the side of the building, and up an iron staircase. Sienna turned her head away as she went past the shop window in case the owner saw her and recognised her.

She'd visited Nick's flat often when

she'd been engaged to him but never alone. He'd always seemed uneasy when they'd been there and would never answer the phone if it rang. Now she slipped the key into the lock and quickly let herself inside.

The flat looked much as it always had done — dusty, very untidy and smelling slightly of damp. But it didn't look un-lived in.

The newspaper on the coffee table was only two days old. Sienna moved quickly over to the old table that Nick always used as a desk. She tried to walk quietly so that the people in the shop wouldn't hear her. She found that she was holding her breath and that her heart was beating too fast and she stopped for a moment to take a deep breath and calm herself. Then she began sorting through the papers on the table.

It looked pretty much the sort of stuff that someone who bought and sold cars might have. There was a stack of log books, a couple of MOT certificates, a pile of keys on cheap plastic rings, a thick stack of old auction lists and many sheets torn from a notebook written in Nick's spiky hand with lists of cars and prices on them.

There were also several newspapers folded into wads with red rings around cars advertised in the auto section. As she replaced everything, Sienna noticed a small drawer in the front of the table. It had no knob so she put her hand flat underneath it and eased it out.

In it were three boxes of pills. Two were unopened and one had just two flat foil packs left in it. Sienna read the long name on the box but it made no sense to her. There was no sticky label with dose instructions and the patient's name. Carefully, she took one of the blister packs and slipped it into her pocket.

She looked around the room again but there was no other place to hide anything. The bedroom and bathroom were likewise. She started for the door, relieved to be leaving, but as she reached it, the phone rang. The noise was shockingly loud in the quiet flat and she whipped round as if she'd been discovered snooping. There was a click and Nick's voice said, 'Nick here. Leave a message.'

A man's voice said, 'It'll be Saturday, Nick. It's a big one. Only overnight. Sort the interfering cow out by then will you? I don't want any muck-ups.' The phone clicked again and the line went dead.

Sienna turned and went out, locking it behind her. The picture was becoming clearer every day, and it was obvious that soon she must confront Nick before he dragged Ashenbourne farm into anything dangerous or illegal. But Abby would only construe Sienna's actions as jealousy or revenge and be drawn more closely to Nick.

As she got into the Mini and drove off, there was only one person that Sienna wanted to talk to. One person who seemed to set her straight. One person who made her feel safe.

Accordingly, she swung the car round and set out for the next village where Leo had his pottery place. She hoped he wouldn't mind her arriving out of the blue. She urgently needed to show him the tablets and tell him about the call on the answering machine.

As she drove nearer to where Leo was,

Sienna felt herself tensing in anticipation of seeing him again.

Smiling to herself, she swung into the courtyard of the old mill where Leo had his pottery. Leo was standing in the middle of the yard. Hanging on to his arm and gazing adoringly up at him was the most beautiful woman that Sienna had ever seen.

8

Sienna stopped the car and got out slowly. Leo and the woman walked over to where she stood, but the woman didn't let go of Leo's arm.

'I'm sorry to bother you, Leo,' Sienna started. 'But I need to talk to you rather urgently. Something's happening on Saturday night and . . . '

Leo interrupted her. His voice was polite but distant. 'This is Anita, Sienna. She's driven up from London today, and bought just about everything in the showroom for her gallery in London. Anita, this is Sienna. She's an acquaintance of mine.'

Sienna managed a small, fake smile. Acquaintance. With wind-blown hair and no make-up. Not like the woman hanging on to him, with her perfect pearly teeth, wide-apart blue eyes and tinted hair done up on top of her perfect head.

'I'd like to talk, Sienna,' continued Leo, 'But Anita wants me to make some special pots, and take them to London at the weekend. It's rather a large order so we need to get on. Can we talk some other time?'

'Of course.' Sienna got back into her car and started it. As she put it into gear she heard Leo say, 'Sorry about that.'

Back at the farm all was quiet. The housekeeper was obviously out and Nick and Abby would still be in London. Sienna made tea and took it up to her bedroom. The existence of Leo had been such a comfort to her lately that now, after his brusque treatment of her, she felt abandoned and totally alone.

She got on to her bed and curled up with her old teddy under her chin as usual. Then she remembered the tablets and got up and hid them in a jar on her dresser. Back on the bed she let the phone message she had overheard run over and over in her head. She knew what she was going to have to do, but now she was going to have to do it alone.

She had counted so much on Leo's support to get her through the current mess, and now he was turning his back because some gorgeous woman wanted him and his pottery. She let a wry smile escape on to her lips and told herself that there were few men who could resist making money, and if this included a beautiful woman obviously fancying you, it must be totally irresistible.

Nick and Abby arrived home about seven. Sienna heard the car pull up and steeled herself for another evening of Abby's hostility and Nick's complacency. But Abby came straight upstairs calling Sienna's name and then burst into her room loaded with bags, smiling.

'Oh I had a lovely time, Sienna. We went to loads of shops and had lunch in a restaurant where they had live lobsters in tanks!' She sat down on the bed and pulled a blue jumper out of one of the bags and held it up against her. 'Does this suit me?'

'Yes, it does.' Sienna was astonished to see Abby back to her normal self. 'It looks really nice. How come you're not cross with me any more?'

'Oh that! Nick talked to me about it in the car on the way back from London. He says he probably over reacted that day in the kitchen and you were probably just larking about. He wants us to be friends again so we can all live here together happily. I've been really miserable while we've not been friends. Hug?'

Sienna reached over and gave her sister a long hug. Then while Abby prattled happily on about her trip and displayed her shopping, Sienna tried to think what Nick had up his sleeve this time.

Admittedly it would be easier living together if the two girls were friends, but there had to be more to it than that. 'And guess what?' Abby continued.

'He's planned an outing for us on Saturday night. Tickets to the theatre at Nottingham. We always used to go. Do you remember?'

'Yes, but he should have told me. I'm afraid I've got plans to meet a friend of mine on Saturday evening.' Sienna was thinking fast. Much as she hated lying to Abby, it would be most beneficial if Nick thought she was far away on Saturday night.

He obviously wanted it that way, hence the theatre plans, but Sienna had plans that didn't include having Abby with her and she was not going to give them up. 'I think I might stay the night too. It's a long drive.' Abby's face fell so Sienna hurried on. 'I'll tell Nick and we'll go some other evening to the theatre shall we?'

Dinner that evening was a much more cheerful affair than it had been for a long time. Mrs McKenna had left her famous Lancashire hotpot in the Aga and fresh strawberries and cream for afters. Abby chatted happily throughout the meal and helped Sienna load the dishwasher afterwards.

Nick was quiet and seemed preoccupied. Sienna couldn't help wondering what his business had been in London, and just what was happening on Saturday night. Later, they watched TV in the lounge until about nine o'clock when Sienna got up and announced her intention to take Patch for his usual evening walk.

Abby got up too, and said she would like to go, but Nick held out his arms. 'Oh don't go. Come and have a cuddle.' Soon she was settled on the sofa with him.

Sienna went out into the kitchen, called Patch from the dairy where he slept most of the day on his master's now-unused bed, and went out of the back door. It was just starting to get dark, but Sienna had lived on the farm all her life and knew the footpaths and fields like the back of her hand.

Soon she and Patch were heading up the narrow track to the copse that her father and mother had planted thirty years before. A chill little wind sprung up and Sienna hugged her shirt around her as she walked.

It was Patch who gave the alarm. Suddenly he stopped dead and growled deep in his throat. Sienna stopped too, wondering what was wrong with him. There was a sudden rustling of the nearest bushes and she felt herself gripped firmly from behind, with her arms pinned to her sides. Patch was not a vicious dog by nature and he seemed as frightened as Sienna as he rushed round and round in circles, barking and whining.

Whoever had hold of Sienna smelled awful. It was a combination of old sweat, alcohol and unwashed clothes. When he put his mouth to her ear she felt a hard stubble against her cheek. She screamed just once in fear and surprise then set about kicking backwards at the legs of the man who held her.

'None of that!' He twisted her in his

grasp so that his legs were safe from her heels. Patch rushed forwards and threw himself at the man's legs but he received a swift kick as his reward and ran back out of the way, crying.

'For God's sake, what do you want?' Sienna screamed. 'I haven't got any money on me. Let me go!' She squirmed and fought but was unable to break free, so she put her head down and bit as hard as she could at the hand that was holding her shoulder.

In return she received a hard slap to the side of her head and felt the gold chain that had been her mother's ripped from her neck. Dazed from the blow, she stood still while her attacker wrenched the matching gold bracelet from her wrist, then set about trying to get the signet ring off her right hand.

Sienna knew that if this was a robbery the best thing she could do was let the thief have what he wanted so that he would go away, so she stood still. Suddenly, she heard feet pounding up the track and Nick's voice yelled,

'Let her go, you creep. Who the hell are you? Let her go, I said.'

The man holding Sienna let go and ran up the track towards the copse. Nick took off after him and Sienna fell numbly to her knees. After a moment she knelt beside poor Patch and tried to comfort him.

Two minutes later Abby came panting up the path from the house. 'Oh Sienna! What was it? Nick suggested we had a walk too, and we were just at the bottom of the track when we heard Patch barking. Has someone hurt you? What happened?'

Sienna got shakily to her feet. 'Someone robbed me, Abby, that's all. I'm not hurt but he took Mum's chain bracelet and he kicked poor Patch when he tried to defend me. Where's Nick gone? Can you help me get Patch to the house and we'll call the police and the vet.'

'I hope Nick's all right.' Abby was peering up the track. 'Oh isn't he brave to go running after someone in the dark. He could be huge, or have a gun or a knife.'

Sienna was thinking much the same, and was puzzled by Nick's new bravado. The previous year he had been mugged outside a tube station in London and had recounted with pride how speedily he had handed over his wallet and run away. Now he rushed after unknown men in the dusk. At that moment he came back, breathing heavily and limping slightly.

'Here you go, Sienna.' He held out his hand and gave Sienna the bracelet and chain. 'The chain's broken. I had a bit of a struggle to get it off him, but I did finally. I just couldn't hang on to him. I chased him as far as I could. He'll be long gone by now.'

'Oh Nick, you were so brave,' Abby breathed, and rushed to hug him. Together, the three of them got Patch back to the farmhouse and rang the police and the vet.

The vet was local and came almost immediately. She felt Patch's ribs and declared nothing broken, but said that he would be sore and bruised for a week or so. The policeman arrived some time later, and took statements from all three. He walked outside and up the track but found nothing.

'We don't usually get that sort of trouble this far out,' he remarked as he closed his notebook. 'Perhaps someone passing through. I'll get a constable to drive by on his rounds for a week or so.' After making sure that Sienna was unharmed, he left.

Nick, Abby and Sienna sat at the kitchen table where they could keep an eye on Patch. Nick produced a bottle of cognac and glasses and poured three drinks. Leo's warning popped into Sienna's head but she was far too shaken to care and anyway, all three drinks came out of the same bottle and were poured in front of her.

'What a good job Nick suggested we come for a walk with you,' Abby said, 'I hate to think what might have happened if he hadn't arrived when he did.'

'I thought you looked quite comfortable when I left,' Sienna replied. 'What changed your mind?'

'Must by psychic or something.' Nick downed his cognac. 'But one thing's for sure. You girls need a man around this place. Tonight has proved that. I think if anyone had any ideas about Abby and I leaving, this should put paid to them don't you? I thought for a while that Leo was going to be around but he seems to have vanished into thin air.'

'He's going to London this weekend,' Sienna said unhappily. 'I don't think I'll be seeing him again.'

'See what I mean? I think I need to be around in case that bloke comes back. There'll be no-one robbing people and making vile threats while I'm around, that's for sure.'

Abby said again, 'Oh you are so brave, Nick.'

And Sienna thought, 'That's funny. I was so shaken I don't think I mentioned the threats.'

9

By Saturday, Sienna was a bag of nerves but she was determined to carry out her plan. When no-one was about, she slipped a dark suede coat, a plaid travel rug and a thermos full of coffee into her car ... At five in the afternoon she went into the living room where Nick and Abby were watching TV and said her goodbyes. She'd packed a small overnight bag to cover her story and she carried it with her.

'Definitely staying the night, are you then?' Nick asked lazily.

'Yes. Be back at lunchtime tomorrow.'

'Have a lovely time, Sienna. I'll miss you.' Abby came and gave her a kiss and Sienna felt mean and deceitful for lying to someone so trusting. But some things had to be done. All she had to do now was kill some time until she and

Abby would have left for the theatre in Nottingham had they taken up Nick's offer.

She had worked out that whatever was going to happen was going to happen between seven-thirty when they would have left, and eleven-thirty when they would have arrived home. She felt a very real fear leaving Abby and had to keep telling herself that she really wasn't going to be away all night.

She drove off at seven, but soon doubled back via a narrow lane, one that was used in the past to take the sheep down to the village. She parked the Mini in an open gateway, got the flask and the rug out of the car, put on her suede coat, and climbed the low stone wall on to the lower field of Ashenbourne Farm.

It was a stiff hike up the hill but it brought her round the back of the barns and to a small fallen-down stone cairn on the top field. From here she had a perfect view of the barnyard and anything that came or went into it.

She folded the rug into a pad and sat down on the ground and waited. It was dusk just after eight-thirty tonight, with the moon starting to be obscured by drifting clouds. Every fifteen minutes Sienna got up and strolled back down the field to stretch her legs. By ten-thirty she was very stiff and very, very bored. But still she waited.

At ten-forty she heard a heavy engine in the distance. When she stood up she could see a set of headlights swinging off the main road on to the farm lane. The lights were a long way off the ground and it seemed to be a very big vehicle indeed, judging by the deep sound of its engine.

At the same moment, a hand was clamped over her mouth and she was grabbed from behind. A dreadful feeling of déjà vu swept over her and as before, she tried to struggle. But the arms that held her were like iron and the hand over her mouth was immovable.

'I'll take my hand away but say you

won't shout first,' said Leo's voice. He removed his hand and Sienna turned within the circle of his arms and felt a wonderful surge of joy to find herself there. Leo released her and stood back. 'Sorry, Sienna. I couldn't see who it was and I didn't want to take a chance that it was a look-out Nick had posted. Are you all right?'

'Yes, I'm fine. But I thought you were in London.'

'Delivering pottery to the lovely Anita?'

'That's what you said.'

'I know. Look, sit down here where we can see what's coming into the yard. I don't know what it is but it's going quite slowly.' He sank to the ground and Sienna did the same. 'But there was a problem,' he continued. 'The lovely Anita turned up out of the blue saying how much she loved my pottery and how she wanted a huge consignment for her London gallery and would I deliver it.'

'Well?'

'The problem was that when I asked her what she planned to retail them at it, turned out she had no idea what wholesale and retail prices were. And when I mentioned V.A.T., her eyes glazed over. If she runs a gallery, I'll eat my hat!'

'And?'

'And I concluded that someone was setting me up. I think had I gone hot-footing down to London with a vanload of pots, I might just have found I had to deliver to an address that didn't exist. And from that, I concluded that someone wanted me out of Ashenbourne this weekend.'

'Huh. That someone wanted me gone too. He even bought tickets to the theatre, but that would have meant I had Abby with me, so I pretended I was going to stay with a friend.'

'And then you nearly blew the whole thing out of the water, arriving at the pottery and blurting out your suspicions. Fortunately, whatever actress or barmaid had agreed to set me up,

106

didn't know you from Adam, so I just played cool and pretended you were just an acquaintance.'

'Are you saying what I think you're saying?'

'Probably. I assume the someone who wants me out of the way is Nick. And I assume that if he'll go to the trouble of paying someone to set me up, he must have something big going down.'

'He has,' said Sienna. 'I went to his flat and I heard someone on his answering machine saying that something big was going down this Saturday night. And I found pills, Leo. I don't know what they are, but I can hazard a good guess. No wonder Abby has been so dopey. Oh, poor Abby.'

By now the big vehicle was in the barnyard and they could see that it was a massive yellow agricultural machine. There was a grinding, sliding sound and Sienna said, 'Well, that's the big doors of the steel barn. Perhaps we're wrong, Leo. Perhaps Nick's taking up farming.'

Both of them smiled in the darkness. More lights were coming down the farm lane. Soon a flat-bred truck with a smart little yacht on its back swung into the yard and was driven into the barn.

'Good gracious,' said Leo. 'He wasn't kidding about a big consignment, was he? I wonder if that's the lot?'

It wasn't. Twenty minutes later, a new-looking white motor home appeared at the yard and disappeared into the barn. Then they heard shouting, and the rasping sound of the steel doors sliding shut. An ordinary car engine started up and they watched it drive away from the farm, presumably carrying the drivers of the delivered vehicles.

'Phew!' Sienna let her breath out. 'Nick seems to be deviating from buying cars.'

'He's not bought these, Sienna. They're on their way to buyers who've had them stolen to order, I bet. I don't think Nick could handle robbery on this scale. No, he's just renting out your barns to the thieves until they can deliver them to the people for whom they've stolen them.'

'Ugh! What a filthy business. Let's call the police, shall we?'

'Yes, we will. But something's bothering me. This is all a bit brazen, even for Nick. You could have decided to come home early and arrived in the middle of it all. He seems a bit sure of himself. I think we'll go down and have a word with him. I want to know why he thinks he can get away with all this. He's got to get rid of them too, don't forget. How is he planning that? He can't bank on you being gone all the time.'

Leo picked up the blanket and he and Sienna made their way down to the farmhouse. As they approached, they could hear a muffled barking from the window of the old dairy.

'Patch is locked in again,' muttered Sienna.

They came in through the back door into the lighted kitchen. Nick was standing at the refrigerator, his head tilted back, drinking a beer out of the can. When he saw Leo and Sienna he froze in that position as if he couldn't believe his eyes. Then he choked on the beer.

Leo strode round the table, took the beer, grabbed Nick by the scruff of the neck and plonked him down in one of the kitchen chairs. He was at least six inches taller than Nick and twice as muscular, so Nick sat where he had been put and glowered up at Leo. Sienna went through into the old dairy. Patch was shut in the walk-in cupboard. She let him out and came back into the kitchen.

'Fun and games in the barn tonight, eh, Nick?' Leo placed a kitchen chair next to Nick, turned it round and sat down astride with his arms folded across its back. 'Right. Let's hear it. I want to know what you're up to. You've got three probably stolen vehicles in the big barn and I know this has been going on for a while. I also think you've been dosing the girls with something so they won't hear your goings-on at night and

I also think you tried to get rid of the old dog so it wouldn't bark and wake their father up when he was alive. So what have you got to say about that then?'

To Sienna's astonishment, Nick leaned back in his chair, took cigarettes and a lighter out of his shirt pocket and lit up. 'Well, if that's what you think, go into the hall, pick up the phone and call the police.'

He seemed so calm, so sure of himself, that Sienna thought, Leo's right. He's got something up his sleeve.

'You don't care if I call the police, Nick? You, with a barn full of stolen vehicles?'

'Me? A barn? I haven't got a barn, Leo. I just stay here. Now, Sienna — she's the one with a barn.'

Leo was silent. Sienna could tell that he was suddenly worried. She came forward. 'That's no problem, Leo. We can both vouch for the fact I knew nothing about it. Go and make the call.'

Leo held up a hand. 'Nick doesn't

seem too worried about me calling the police, Sienna,' he said thoughtfully. 'I wonder why that is? Why is that, Nick?'

Nick took a deep drag on his cigarette and blew the smoke into Leo's face. 'Oh, nothing,' he said. 'It's got nothing to do with me. Now, Abby. That's a different matter.'

Sienna felt her blood run cold. She realised that she had forgotten that Abby was at the farmhouse, and without saying anything else, she ran out of the kitchen and up the stairs.

Abby was in bed, sleeping deeply and would not wake up. Sienna covered her over with the duvet and went back downstairs again.

'I'm going to call a doctor, Leo, and see just what he's given her. She's dead asleep, so he can get on with his shady little deal without her knowing.' She turned to go out to the hall but Nick's voice called her back.

'I wouldn't fetch the police or a doctor, Sienna. If you do, I might have to produce all the documents she's

112

signed. Oh, and the prescription pads she stole while she was working at the doctor's surgery. Might not go too well for her.'

'She wouldn't do that.' But Sienna's voice trembled.

'A girl will do anything when she's in love. She does anything I tell her and she just signs anything I give her. Of course, the blokes who have put the stuff into the barns don't sign contracts. No, what Abby's signed is more of an offer to rent, but it states quite plainly that the barns are to be used for storing stolen stuff. I should know — I wrote it.' He looked at their horrified faces. 'Oh, come on,' he continued. 'We all know that Abby isn't the sharpest tack in the box, don't we?'

Sienna walked slowly over to where Nick sat, drew back her arm and backhanded him across the face. Nick would have jumped up but was restrained by Leo. 'Well done, Sienna,' he said. 'He deserved that.'

Nick recovered quickly. 'I don't see

you rushing to the phone, Sienna.'

'No. I can't and you know I can't. But I can tell you this, Nick. From now on I'm not leaving her side. I'm going to tell her everything I know about you and let her make up her own mind. You get that stuff out of the barns and don't you ever bring any of your rotten, stolen stuff here again.

'You're leaving as soon as the barns are empty and you're never coming on to this farm again.' Nick tried to interrupt, but Sienna carried on. 'I want you out of this house and out of our lives and you can go and crawl right back into whichever slimy little hole you crawled out of. If Abby decides she wants to go with you, I can't stop her, but I'm hoping she'll see sense when I tell her all I know.'

'Oh, she'll come with me, Sienna. Don't worry about that. You see, she loves me, bless her simple little heart.'

'Oh, why don't you go away and leave us alone,' Sienna burst out. 'I wish I could just wave a magic wand and have you disappear out of our lives for ever.'

Nick sat up. 'Now, there's an interesting proposition,' he said thoughtfully. 'A magic wand. As a matter of fact, Sienna, you have got a magic wand that can make me disappear for ever.'

'I have?'

'Yes.'

'Where is it?'

'It's in the bank, darling. Twenty thousand pounds should do the trick.'

10

There was a silence that seemed to go on forever, then Leo said disgustedly, 'Shall I chuck him out, Sienna?'

'No. Do you mean that for twenty thousand pounds you'd leave Abby alone and clear off for good?'

'You are so sharp, Sienna. I've always liked that about you. Yes, a quickie divorce and off into the wild blue yonder. Sound good?'

Sienna sat down at the table. 'Mmmmm . . . and would Abby know about this?'

'Of course not. Who'd tell her? I'd be gone. A clean break.'

'You can't seriously be contemplating this, Sienna!' Leo's voice was harsh.

'Oh, but I am. Not many people can get their lives back for a mere twenty thousand pounds. Dad left me his money and trusted me to keep Abby safe. I can't think of a better way to spend it. It's a deal, Nick.'

Leo tutted with disgust, but Nick sat up and looked pleased with himself. 'I take it a cheque wouldn't be acceptable?' Sienna asked coldly.

'Cash is always so much more friendly.'

'I'll have to go to the bank tomorrow. Get out of here tonight. I just don't want you around. I know you have your flat you can go to. Come back here at twelve tomorrow. In Dad's old office. I want you gone as soon as I hand over the cash.'

'No problem.'

'And doesn't it bother you one little bit that you are going to break Abby's heart?'

'Hmmm. Let me think. Well, that took two seconds. The answer's no.'

'And Abby is going to think that you just dumped her and went off with someone else?'

'Better that than the truth.'

'Yes, I suppose it is, under the

circumstances. So that's settled then. Everything out of the barns tomorrow and you go after I give you the money.'

'Sounds so easy, doesn't it? They are fetching the stuff early in the morning by the way. No need to hide any more now it's out in the open?'

'None at all. So glad we had this little talk. Go now. Oh, and Nick?'

'Yes?'

'What have you given Abby?'

'No need to go into that, Sienna. Just rest assured it won't harm her. She's taken it loads of times without knowing and it's never hurt her. I would never harm her. She'll just have a good night's sleep. Millions of people take what she's taken tonight and suffer no ill effects.'

'I hope you're right. For your sake.'

Nick went out of the kitchen and Leo swung round to face Sienna.

'Are you out of your mind?'

'On the contrary. Never been more in it.'

'You're not going to give that slimy

118

creep the money are you? I'll have no part in this, Sienna.'

'But . . .'

'I'm sorry but I don't agree with what you're doing. On top of everything else you're deceiving Abby and that can never be right. I thought better of you, Sienna!' Leo turned and went out of the door. Sienna heard the front door close behind him, and then his car accelerated away.

★ ★ ★

Sienna did not sleep much that night. The knowledge of what was in the barn, and the sort of people who were concerned with such a venture brought her out in a cold sweat. Half-a-dozen times she woke up thinking she heard a police siren, and imagined a raid on Ashenbourne Farm.

She imagined poor Abby being led away in handcuffs. The image of Leo's shocked and disapproving face haunted her, and the knowledge that he thought so little of her filled her with sorrow.

At five a.m. she heard the engines start up in the barnyard, and the vehicles were moved out. While she gritted her teeth to think that she was allowing the stolen stuff to go on its way without hindrance, she breathed a sigh of relief that it was no longer her problem.

She was at the bank at nine-thirty when it opened, and back at the farm by ten. She made tea and took it up to Abby in bed. When she finally roused her she looked straight into her eyes and said, 'You have to get up and get dressed, Abby. There's something we have to do.'

Abby's voice was whiney. 'I feel awful. Where's Nick?'

'He had something he had to do. Get up now and get dressed.'

At twelve, Sienna was sitting in her father's chair in his old office in the dairy. It was the first time she'd done so since his death and it felt strange but vaguely comforting. She took the wad of money out of its envelope and laid it on the desk in front of her. The price of a broken heart.

She heard Nick's car arrive a minute after twelve. He came jauntily across the room and perched on the edge of the desk. He seemed unable to take his eyes off the thick wad of money.

'Right,' said Sienna. 'Let's just run through this again shall we to make sure we understand each other.' She tapped the money with the flat of her hand. 'Twenty thousand. And in exchange you promise to go away, leave my sister alone, and never come back again. Are we clear?'

'Perfectly.'

'And never breathe a word of it to her.'

'Not a word.'

'And divorce her as quickly as possible?'

'As fast as I can.'

Sienna picked up the banknotes. Nick's hand was stretched out ready but instead of handing them over to

Nick she put them in her bag.

Nick said, 'Hey, what's the deal . . . ?' and Sienna said quietly. 'You can come out now, Abby.'

Abby stepped out of the walk-in cupboard where Sienna had put her fifteen minutes before. Her face was white. She came slowly across the room to where Nick sat, frozen, on the edge of the desk.

'I just didn't believe her, Nick. I thought you were playing a trick on HER and would turn the tables at the last minute. But she was right. You were actually going to take the money weren't you? You were going to leave me without a word and divorce me for this . . . bundle of money. Surely our life together was worth more than just money? What an idiot I must be, I really thought you loved me.'

Her voice broke and Nick had the grace to look ashamed. He got up and hurried out. Sienna put her arms around Abby but her sister pushed her off. 'Oh no, Sienna. I'm not going to cry. I'm going to be grown-up and sensible about this. I'll just get on with my life and let Nick get on with his. He'll come to his senses one day just you wait and see. He wouldn't have married me if he didn't feel something for me surely? I may not be bright like you but I'm not totally unlovable am I?'

'Of course not. You are a kind, wonderful person and everyone loves you. But after what you saw today you probably shouldn't be thinking about a future with Nick,' Sienna said softly. 'In fact I can't believe that you would ever even speak to him again.'

'That's the difference between you and me, Sienna. You give up too easily. Nick's my husband. I can't just end my marriage because he goes off the rails a bit. I like being married. It made me feel like everyone else instead of just dumpy old Abby. Oh well, I'll just have to look after myself until he comes to his senses.'

'We'll look after each other,' said Sienna, hugging her sister. 'I've already asked Mrs McKenna to stay over for a few nights. I didn't know quite what was going to happen. I've asked her to make us something special for dinner.'

'Well then I won't be sad or angry any more,' Abby said. 'I wish Leo was here. I always feel so safe whenever he's near. He's a different sort of man isn't he?'

'Very different.' Sienna agreed. As she spoke her heart squeezed painfully in her chest and a wave of longing swept over her.

'Did he know what you were going to do? With me and Nick, I mean?'

'No,' said Sienna. 'He actually thought I was going to pay Nick twenty thousands pounds to desert you. I was so cross that he would think that of me. I let him go home thinking I would do that awful thing.'

'I think you should let him know, Sienna. It's not nice having people you love thinking bad things about you.'

Sienna looked sharply at Abby. 'Love?'

'Oh yes,' Abby replied. 'I know you

very well. You're bonkers about Leo. And I don't blame you. That sort of man doesn't come along often.' She added sadly.

'I'll ring him then,' Sienna said suddenly, and got up and went out into the hall to find the phone book.

Leo answered on the first ring.

'Hello?'

'Leo? It's Sienna. I'm ringing to tell you that I didn't give Nick the money, nor did I have any intention of doing so. I hid Abby in the room and let her hear the deal. I just wanted you to know, that's all.'

'Why?'

'Because . . . because . . . I couldn't bear to have you thinking badly of me.'

There was silence. 'Listen,' Leo said softly. 'I want you to be very careful. Nick's a nasty bit of work and he'll be furious. Promise me you won't do anything silly. I just couldn't bear it if anything happened to you.'

Sienna hung up the phone, her heart singing.

★ ★ ★

That evening, things felt almost back to normal. At eight, the housekeeper produced a splendid beef stew for dinner, and crème caramel for dessert. She had moved into the dairy for the few days she had been asked to stay, and she retired there after she had prepared the dinner. Sienna opened a bottle of red wine and poured for herself and Abby. Halfway through dinner Abby solemnly raised her glass.

'Here's to sisters,' she said. 'And sheepdogs. And memories of lovely fathers. And . . . efficient housekeepers . . . and . . . and . . .'

'Ancient farmhouses . . . and . . . old teddy bears . . . and . . .' Sienna hesitated, thinking.

'Big gorgeous men with bright green eyes and horrible scowls,' Abby shouted. Both girls burst into helpless laughter. Patch barked his approval from his basket. And then the phone rang.

Sienna took it in the hall. Nick's

voice sounded slurred, as if he was drunk. 'Glad I caught you, Sienna. Not a very nice trick you played at lunchtime, was it? I thought you were a person of your word.'

Sienna recovered from her surprise at hearing Nick's voice. 'I am,' she said. 'But not when I'm dealing with slimeballs. What do you want? I'm busy.'

'Just thought I'd ask you if you'd seen your boyfriend, Leo lately.'

'He isn't my boyfriend and no I haven't seen him. What's it to do with you anyway? Go away. I'm hanging up now.'

'Oh I've already gone away darling. I'm miles away I promise. But before I left I stopped into your boyfriend's little pottery place. Oh no, don't worry. He didn't see me. It was just that there was this lovely storeroom full of boxes and packing right under the flat where he lives and well, you see, he's been an awful bully to me, so . . . '

'What have you done, Nick? Tell me!'

'Oh don't worry, Sienna. It's far too late for you to do anything about it. It was about three hours ago when I had my little accident with the lighted cigarette. The fire engine was pretty quick off the mark but the place looked pretty well alight when I left. And the problem was, I wedged something in front of his door so he couldn't get out. Poor, poor Leo.'

There was a click and the line went dead.

11

Sienna ran back to the kitchen, shouted, 'Stay with Mrs McKenna, Abby. I have to go out!' and rushed out to her car. It should have taken half-an-hour to reach the next village, but Sienna wasn't bothering about speed limits. Foremost in her mind was one thing — Leo's life was in danger because of what she'd done and suddenly the idea of a world without Leo seemed unthinkable. Screeching around bends and roaring up lanes, she arrived outside the old mill expecting to see fire engines and police cars, smoke and flame, and people rushing back and forth.

Instead, nothing moved in the old mill. The building was totally quiet and dark. Sienna sat in her car, unable to believe what she was seeing. Obviously, Nick had been lying. But why? What was the point? Revenge to pay her back for tricking him over the money? What was the point? It just seemed too petty. And then suddenly it struck her like a dash of cold water. She had come running out and left Abby at home with just the housekeeper!

Frantic with worry at her own stupidity, she got out of the car and ran up the metal stairs to Leo's flat and banged on the door. Nobody moved and all was dark. Leo was not home. Quickly, Sienna pulled out her mobile phone and dialled the farm. No-one answered.

There was only one thing to do. Swiftly, she ran back to her car and set off for home. As she turned out of the lane where Leo lived, another car switched on its lights behind her and started to follow.

As there was often traffic on that road, Sienna didn't worry. However the car stayed behind her as she drove too fast in the direction of the farm, and was close behind her when she turned on to the main Ashenbourne Road.

With mounting horror she saw the car behind come closer and closer at high speed. Suddenly, the Mini lurched violently forward. Sienna heard the crunch and felt a violent pain in her neck, but fortunately the Mini had a headrest and her head only banged against it instead of whiplashing. She instinctively put her foot down on the accelerator, but the other car seemed to keep up and the next minute rammed the Mini again. This time Sienna had to struggle to keep the little car going straight.

There was an awful tearing, screeching sound of brakes as the other car corrected itself, and then she was free and surging ahead again. She heard her mobile phone ringing in her bag but it meant nothing. All that mattered was staying on the road.

It seemed as if the nightmare would never end. Every time Sienna got ahead, the other, bigger car would accelerate and ram her from behind.

Each time it was becoming harder and harder to keep on the road. The car behind seemed to be increasing in recklessness and aggression and Sienna feared that the little Mini might just fly apart if subjected to any more of the terrible punishment it was getting.

When the turn for the farm lane came into view, Sienna shouted, 'At last!' and took the turn at a speed she would normally have considered unsafe. Gravel spurted out from under her wheels and she overshot the corner dreadfully, but suddenly she was on the bumpy track and hurtling down to the safety of the farm.

Once over the cattle grid, surely no-one would dare chase her into the farmyard where there were lights. The car behind her seemed to slow, as if aware that she had finally reached safety.

Then she saw the lights in the middle of the road. They were dancing and waving from side to side — one big, one small, and both moving frantically as if trying to attract her attention. Without thinking, Sienna slammed on the brakes. She felt the rear end slide, and the wheels bump on to the grass on the side of the track, but the car slid to a halt a few yards from the cattle grid. Behind her she heard the other car reverse quickly back up the track and accelerate away.

The bobbing lights still approached the car and she could see two shadowy figures. Then her door was yanked violently open and she felt herself lifted bodily out of the car and enfolded in a pair of strong arms.

'Thank God you're safe, Sienna. Oh, what would I have done if anything had happened to you? Who was that chasing you? Where have you been this time of night?' Leo kissed her and this time it was a burning kiss full of longing and promise. Sienna clung to him as reaction set in.

'Are you all right, Sienna?' Abby's voice was worried. 'Where did you go?'

'Put me down,' Sienna demanded.

But still she clung to Leo's arm, revelling in the feel of him. 'What on earth are you doing here?' she asked.

'You first,' Leo said. 'Where did you go haring off to?'

'I went to see you. Nick rang and said he'd set your flat on fire. All I could think of was getting to you.'

Leo held her close and whispered against her hair, 'Nick has gone too far this time. He really meant to give you a nasty shock.'

'Why did you come up the lane to stop me? I was almost home.'

In answer, Leo swung his torch on to the road a few yards in front of where Sienna had finally stopped. It illuminated an eighteen-inch pit in front of the farm's gates. The cattle grid was gone.

12

'Nick must have rung you from his car, watched you leave the farm, and then moved the grid,' Leo said. They were sitting in the living room at the farmhouse. 'He must have had someone with him. It's heavy. Then he waited for you on the road back. I think he's lost his mind. What a dangerous thing to do. It's a shallow pit but you would have had a nasty bump.'

'But why are you here and how did you get here if the grid was up?' Sienna asked.

'I was out making deliveries and I started thinking about what you told me on the phone. I drove up the back way, up the sheep lane, parked and came up the field. I didn't want anyone to see me arrive. I wasn't going to stay long, just wanted to make sure you were both locked in safe for the night.

'When I got here Abby and Mrs McKenna were both trying to find out what Patch was barking about. We got torches and decided to come out and see what was the matter. Patch led us straight to the gate and we saw that the grid was missing. We tried to phone you but got no answer.'

'Good old Patch,' said Abby. Patch was sitting on the floor at her feet and he thumped his tail happily.

'Nick must hate me very much,' Sienna said sadly.

'His sort don't like being outwitted. Especially by a woman,' Leo said. 'I think we're going to have to be very careful in future. There's no telling what he'll do. We should probably call the police.'

'I just can't believe Nick would do something so stupid,' said Abby. 'He knows how much I love Sienna. I don't think he'd try to hurt her. And anyway, he'll just deny it. He always does if things go wrong. And we haven't got any proof at all. Oh I wish he wouldn't do such awful things. You shouldn't have made him cross, Sienna.'

Suddenly Sienna felt extremely tired and discouraged. The desperate dash back to the farm had taken its toll on her nerves and now her eyes were closing and her head nodding. Leo told her to go to bed and said that he would lock up and make all secure.

The relief of handing over responsibility to someone so able to handle it was enormous, and she went gratefully upstairs and fell into her bed. She heard the housekeeper letting Leo out of the front door, and then heard various sounds that told her he was checking the outside of the house. Finally, a small shower of gravel hit her window and she got up and opened it. Leo stood under her window, the moonlight lighting up his pale hair.

'I'll go and get someone to help me to put the grid back so if you hear a car that's what it will be. Otherwise, if anyone rings you, it doesn't matter who they say they are, don't go out of the house will you?'

'All right,' said Sienna. 'Goodnight Leo.'

Then she snuggled down under her old quilt and remembered him lifting her out of the car, and the trembling of his hands when he touched her. The memory was so vivid that she shivered slightly in her warm bed, and murmured his name as she fell asleep.

* * *

Sienna slept late the following morning and it was nine-thirty before she came downstairs into the kitchen. She had expected to find Abby there but the housekeeper said she hadn't seen her. She went back upstairs but found Abby's bed empty. It was puzzling. Abby sometimes stepped outside with Patch in the mornings so Sienna hurried downstairs again and opened the back door to look for her.

With all that going on, she didn't feel safe unless she knew where Abby was.

The phone rang in the hall as she went back into the kitchen and she rushed to answer it. The line was very bad and kept cutting out but there was no mistaking Abby's voice. She sounded close to tears and Sienna gripped the receiver tightly.

'Sienna?'

'Yes? Where are you?'

'I'm in a car. I'm on my way to London. I'm very sorry but this is the way it has to be. Please don't worry about me. It'll be all right. And will you look after Patch?'

Sienna thought she might scream. 'Whose car?' she said. She tried to make her voice calm. 'Why are you going to London?'

'Because that's where Nick's friend's flat is. He says he can't live in Ashenbourne any more with everything that's gone on. He says he didn't take the grid up and he didn't chase you in his car. I told you he wouldn't do that but you didn't believe me. And he only phoned you about the fire at Leo's to

139

pay you back for cheating him about the money. He's really sorry about that.'

'He's a liar, Abby. Oh why are you with him? How did you get to him?'

'I rang him last night after you were in bed. He picked me up at the top of the lane early this morning. I'm sorry, Sienna but this is what I have to do.'

'But Abby. After all the things he's done.'

'He says you have no proof he did any of those things. And anyway, things are different now that . . . I'll ring you when we get to London and give you an address. I'll need you to send me some money if you don't mind.'

'But why, Abby? Why are you doing this?'

There was a rustling sound as if the phone had changed hands and then Nick's cocky voice came on the line.

'Hello, sis! Now don't go rushing for the police or anything will you? Abby's coming with me quite willingly aren't you babe? I haven't got a gun to her head or anything. She packed her little bag and walked up the lane to meet me so forget about kidnap. Just send her some money, just to be getting along with — the rent's quite overdue where we're going — and if you're really co-operative, I'll let her ring you every now and then to tell you how she is. Of course, we'll probably need quite a bit of money from you in the future. You know how expensive everything is.'

'What are you doing, Nick? How have you persuaded her to go with you?'

'Her choice I assure you. As I said, she rang me. Now don't forget the money will you? We're going to need loads of things. Send us a nice lump of cash.'

'Forget it, Nick. I'll find out what you've done and I'll come and get Abby and this time I'll make sure you're out of her life for good. There's no reason she could possibly want to be with you.'

'Are you sure about that?'

141

Sienna was reminded of another conversation they had had when she got back from Spain. Nick's voice had been gloating then too, as if he was really enjoying himself.

'Positive.'

'But you're forgetting one thing, Sienna.'

'What's that?'

Nick's voice was triumphant. 'Don't tell me she forgot to mention it?'

'Who?'

'Abby.'

'Mention what?'

There was a long pause and then Nick said. 'The baby.'

★   ★   ★

Sienna sat down on the bottom stair and put her head down on her knees. For a while she sat like that, then again put the phone to her ear.

'Nick?'

'Still here, darling. Just pulling into a service station. Abby wants to go and

142

get us a coffee. Off you go darling. See you in a minute. Sorry about that, Sienna. She's gone now. Where were we? Oh yes. The baby. Did that knock the wind out of you a bit?'

'Are you sure? About the baby?'

'Perfectly. She did a test last night. They're dead easy. Even our simple little Abby can do a pregnancy test.'

'But why, Nick? This can't be what you want. You don't love Abby and don't pretend to. What's the point of this? You'll have to pay maintenance you know.'

'Maintenance? Why on earth should I do that? I live with Abby and am the father of the kid. Only absent fathers pay child maintenance. No, there's only one sort of maintenance that's going to be paid.'

'And that is?'

'Well, it's a bit delicate, Sienna.'

'If it's anything to do with you it will be as delicate as a ton of bricks. What is it you want?'

'Money. I'm in a bit of a financial

crisis. And your sister is in a bit of an emotional crisis. So some on, Sis, cough up and you can make the world right for both of us. How about a little monthly support?'

'Send you money every month to stay with Abby?'

'What a turn-around. First you're giving me money to go away and now it's to stay. What about it? Your dad left you enough and that was to take care of Abby too. Don't be such a greedy girl. Spread it around a bit. Couple of thou a month should do nicely. I'd like to keep our girl in the style to which I'd like to become accustomed. Ha! That's quite funny. Hang on and I'll give you the address.' He gave an address in one of the less wealthy areas of London. 'Great talking to you. Oh, and Sienna?'

'Yes?'

'Abby really needs me now. It would be a shame if you took all your crazy accusations to the police or anything like that. I don't think she'd thank you for it. And there's always the problem of those things I've got that she signed and the scrip pads she stole from the doctors. I'd hate to have to bring that up.'

'Yes, I see. You didn't get the money you wanted me to pay you to go away. And so now you've decided to keep her with you and put up with the baby so you can net a nice little sum every month. Have I got it right?'

'Oh Sienna! How cruel you are.'

'Oh don't worry, Nick. I'm not recording this. But listen. I'm coming to London. Now. Today. To your flat. I'm driving down and I'm setting off now. You just be there.'

'Bring a little cash darling. The rent's way in arrears.'

'It's always about money isn't it, Nick?'

'Of course not. I've been madly in love with your sister since the first time I set eyes on her and now I just can't wait until I can get into the role of father, complete with pushchairs, dirty nappies and sleepless nights. I'm just dying to do the school run and listen to Abby blabbing on about baby food and curtains for the nursery. Of COURSE it's about money!'

13

Later, Sienna would remember opening her mouth twice and no sound coming out. She stood in the hall gripping the phone, unable to hang up, or say a word. Finally, she managed to speak.

'Ring me back as soon as Abby gets back, I want to speak to her.'

'Oh all right. But you can't make her change her mind.'

The phone rang after ten minutes. When Abby came on the line Sienna's words came out in a jumble.

'Abby, I can't believe you're having a baby! But it doesn't make any difference. You don't have to go with him or stay with him. Why on earth would you think you had to? You need to be at home with me where I can look after you. I thought we talked about birth control? Why didn't you talk to me about the baby? How long have you known? What sort of life can you give a baby with Nick?'

Abby's voice was stubborn. 'I'll be all right, Sienna. Nick's as pleased as punch and we're going to a friend's flat. He's really not as bad as you make out. A baby needs a family. And you have Leo now so I'd just have been a nuisance anyway. No, this is for the best. Just send me some money and come and see me when . . . '

Her voice dissolved and Sienna thought her heart would break. She told Abby she loved her and finally hung up. Then she sat on the bottom stair and gritted her teeth at the thought of Abby feeling that she and her child would not be welcome in her own home now that Sienna had Leo. The thought was agonising. And a baby!

The very thing that Ashenbourne Farm needed — to carry on its generations as it had done for three hundred years. Then Sienna shed a few hot tears as she thought how close her father had come to seeing his grand-child, and how thrilled and proud he would have been. The thought was unbearable. She picked up her keys from the hall table and headed out to her car.

Traffic on the M1 was awful, and it was three hours before Sienna reached north London. She drove slowly around, frequently consulting her London map and finally pulled up outside a shabby Victorian block of flats on a busy two-lane road. Crossing the road was a nightmare, but finally she stood in front of the row of bells. A name was crossed out and 'Fenwick' written under it.

She rang the bell, the door buzzed immediately, and she went up to the third floor in a smoke-smelling lift. Nick was standing in the doorway of the flat opposite the lift.

'I've sent Abby out to get a few groceries. She's used to a housekeeper so it's going to be a nasty shock to find out what shopping and housework is all about. Come in.'

He stepped back and led Sienna into a large, bare apartment. It smelled of cigarettes and frying food. The carpet was stained and the furniture plain. It was a far cry from the homely, comfortable farmhouse which she and Abby were so used to. Sienna sat down on the settee.

'Right Nick. Let's get business out of the way before Abby gets back shall we? We can dispense with the niceties because we both know what you are and what you want. Well, here it is.'

Sienna took the bulky envelope out of her bag and went and put it on the table in front of Nick who looked at it blankly.

'Money? We've been here before Sienna. Last time it was a trick. What is it this time?'

'It's no trick,' said Sienna quietly. 'This money is for you and Abby. There's forty thousand there. A gift, free and clear. Last time I said the money was yours if you would go. This time it's because you are staying. It's a downpayment on a house or a flat, or years of rent on a flat. It's to make sure that Abby and the baby have everything they need.

'This is our father's money and he trusted me to give it to her when she needed it. Well, she needs it now. I'll make sure there is a regular monthly income as well.'

Nick started to speak but Sienna held up her hand. 'You've made your motives quite plain, Nick. What I'm hoping is that this money will convince you to stay with Abby. You can have a nice place to live and an income, which is what you've wanted all along. Abby gets a place to live, her baby, and her husband which is all she ever wanted. You don't deserve her but there is nothing I can do about that.'

There was the sound of a key in the lock. Nick quickly took the envelope and put it into a drawer on the sideboard. Abby burst into the flat laden with grocery bags which she dropped and flung her arms around Sienna.

'Oh, Sienna. Please don't be cross at my decision. It's time I grew up. This is my life now. Me and Nick and the baby. This flat isn't very nice I know but we'll soon find another one and get it fixed up and have a nursery with nice curtains . . . ' Nick's face contorted. 'And a cot and everything. Goodness, isn't food expensive? I had no idea! I'll make us some tea. You're my first guest. I hope you come to visit all the time.' She bustled off to the kitchen.

Sienna looked at Nick. 'Are we agreed then?' she said.

Nick nodded, but there was a crease in his forehead that Sienna knew well. As she drank her tea and chatted with Abby about the forthcoming baby, she knew that she was going to keep a very close eye indeed on Abby. Finally she stood up.

'I'd like to be home before dark if I can,' she said. The word 'home' brought a mental picture of the old farmhouse, but more importantly, a sudden longing for Leo. In the day's hustle and bustle she had pushed him to the back of her mind but now he came crowding into her head, touching her gently, smelling wonderful, holding her tenderly.

For the first time in her life she shook hands with Nick. She looked him right in the eye and said, 'Take care of her, Nick.' She didn't add, 'or you'll have me to deal with,' but her words implied it

Abby walked her to the lift, and the girls hugged each other hard and promised to stay in touch. As she left the building Sienna felt churned up and uncomfortable.

She kept telling herself that Abby had made the choice for herself and that as her older sister she had to respect it and release the funds to allow it to happen.

At least Abby wasn't going to have to live in a dump and go without things for herself and the baby.

She wished that Abby was more capable of having and taking care of money but that wasn't the case so there was no use wishing for it.

Sighing, Sienna crossed the busy road to her car. She opened the door with relief and was about to get in when she heard her name.

Nick was standing on the other side of the road shouting to her. Puzzled, Sienna waited while he negotiated the fast-moving traffic and rushed over to where she stood.

'Glad I caught you.'

'What's wrong Nick? Is it Abby?'

'Well, in a way.'

'What's happened?'

'Nothing much. It's just that I think she's going to be a bit more expensive than I thought.'

'What on earth are you talking about?'

'Oh, you know. Baby clothes. Prams, toys.' Sienna said nothing. 'And that house you wanted me to put a downpayment on. This is London, Sienna. Property isn't cheap.'

'And?'

'Well, this idea of you giving me a lump sum to stay with Abby and put up with the brat. I'll do it. But not for forty thou.'

'I see. And how much do you want?'

'Hundred thou should do it.'

'I'm sorry, Nick. I thought you realised. The forty thousand was a one-time offer. It isn't negotiable.'

'No?'

'No.'

'Then I guess I'll just take the forty you gave me and go on my own sweet way. Pity. It will just about kill Abby. Oh well. Can't always have things the way we want them.'

'Let me get this straight. You want a hundred thousand pounds of our father's money to stay with Abby and look after her and the baby. If I don't give it to you, you're going to walk out on her?'

'Yup.'

'Without a further thought for her and the baby?'

'Nope.'

'You always were a load of rubbish, Nick Fenwick. And you always will be.

Go and do what you want. If you take the forty and clear off then it's money well spent as far as I'm concerned and good riddance to you. At least I'll honestly be able to tell Abbey I didn't pay you to go this time. You don't think I'd have handed over that sort of money to you without considering the possibility that a little swine like you would take it and leave do you?

'No Nick. This time it's a win-win situation. It would make me very happy if you built a life with Abby with the money. But oh dear how much happier it would make me if you chose to clear off. Do what you want. I hope you do go. Then you can never come back. But be sure about one thing. There's no more money coming your way. A hundred thousand! And you called me greedy!' She bent to open the car door again.

Nick's face darkened. It was plain that he had expected Sienna to give him more money.

'You'll regret this, Sienna. Maybe not

today, but one day. I'll make sure I ruin Abby's life.' He started back across the road, weaving through the fast-moving traffic. 'I'm going back to the flat now to tell her that you tried to pay me to go away again. She'll believe me when I show her the money! She'll never speak to you again. And I'll make sure you NEVER see the baby.'

Out of the corner of her eye Sienna saw the silver off-road vehicle accelerate on the fast lane around the bend and come towards where Nick stood, still shouting over his shoulder. She called, 'Look out, Nick,' but he was too busy looking back at her and having his say.

'And another thing. I'll tell her we've been having an affair ever since you got back from Spain. She'll believe it. She believes anything I tell her. And watch out for that old dog of yours because next time I'll make sure I put it where you NEVER find it.'

Finally he turned back to the road and too late saw the silver car bearing down on him. He hesitated a moment too long, wondering whether to go forwards or backwards, then made a run for it, forwards.

The car hit him square on with its chrome bull bars and cartwheeled him across the road into the central reserve.

He lay there, crumpled like a rag doll. The silver car had neither slowed nor swerved to avoid him, and now it disappeared down the fast lane out of sight. Other motorists screeched to a halt, some pulling out mobile phones.

Sienna got into her car, put her head down, and was sick in the gutter. After a few minutes she got out of the car. Someone had stopped the traffic; there was the sound of a siren in the distance and a cluster of people around where Nick lay on the ground. She started to run back to the flat, hoping to get there before Abby came to the window.

14

At midnight, Sienna and Abby came back to the flat. They moved like sleep walkers, arms around each other, lending each other strength. Once in the flat, Sienna warmed soup and made tea and tried to get Abby to eat something. Abby did not speak at all.

They had got to the hospital too late. All that remained to do was to sign forms and make statements. There would be much more paperwork to be done in the future and arrangements made, but tonight, Sienna thought Abby had had enough. Abby ate a little soup and drank her tea obediently, and got into bed. Sienna locked up the flat, put the lights off, and, when she was ready for bed, got in beside her.

For a while the two sisters lay in silence and Sienna thought Abby had gone straight to sleep. Then Abby said drowsily, 'Poor, poor, Nick. He'll never see his baby. Oh it's too awful.' She began to cry softly.

Sienna put her arms around her sister and held her. 'And the baby,' continued Abby. 'It'll never know its father. I tell you, Sienna, Nick might not have been honest all the time but he was too good to end up like that. Did the police say if they caught the car that hit him?'

'Yes,' said Sienna. 'They found it straight away. It was abandoned on the next street. They told me when they came to the hospital.'

'I wonder why it didn't stop?'

'Because it was stolen, Abby.'

'Oh.' There was a long silence after that, until Abby said, 'Why did Nick follow you down to the car when you left?'

Sienna thought very fast. She was determined not to lie to Abby, but also refused to cause her any more pain.

'He wanted to talk to me about the money I brought with me,' she said finally.

'What money?'

'I brought forty thousand pounds with me when I came.'

'Why?' Abby sat up. 'Oh you didn't try to pay him to go away again after I told you I was having the baby and we were going to be together did you? You wouldn't be that mean.'

'No, I promise you. I brought the money because Nick said he wanted to stay with you and have the baby. It was a downpayment on a house or a flat. That's the truth. Dad would have wanted you to have it. It's yours by right, Abby.'

'But if you'd already given it to him, why did he come running after you when you left?'

Sienna gritted her teeth. 'He said he didn't want that amount,' she said slowly, choosing her words carefully.

'It IS rather a lot of money,' Abby said thoughtfully.

'Anyway, I told him to keep it.'

'Is it still here?'

'Yes. In the sideboard.'

'Hmmm.' Abby was silent for a few minutes then she burst out, 'Oh let's go home tomorrow, Sienna. I want to go home! I don't want to be in London. I want to have my baby at home — not in some horrid flat. And I want you there to look after me, instead of someone telling me to mind my own business all the time and telling me how stupid I am.

'I know Nick loved me in his own sort of way, but the idea of having to run a home and look after the baby with just Nick to rely on was a bit frightening I must confess. But I think he loved me a little bit, don't you, Sienna?'

'I don't know how anyone could NOT love you,' said Sienna, neatly avoiding the question. 'Are you sure about going home?'

'Oh yes. I feel all funny and all at sea, as if I'm living in a dream where horrible things keep happening. I want to be back to normal, as much as things can ever be normal what with the baby coming. I want to see Patch and walk around the farm land and . . . and . . . feel safe and happy. It seems like a long time since I felt like that. Since before you went to Spain.

Safe and happy. Sienna thought of Leo and realised that he made her feel both of those things. She slipped out of bed and went to the phone. Leo picked up on the first ring and Sienna felt stronger at the sound of his voice.

'Leo, it's me. Can you come to the farmhouse tomorrow? I'm afraid that a lot has happened and none of it very good news.'

'As long as you're all right, Sienna. Your housekeeper said you had to leave suddenly. Come home safe, and tell me all about it when you get there.'

'I'll ring you from the car tomorrow and let you know what time we'll be home. See you then.'

Then Sienna got back into bed, cuddled up to Abby and whispered, 'Yes. Let's go home.'

* ★ ★

Early next morning, Sienna and Abby left the flat. The central reserve was cordoned off with yellow tape and both girls studiously averted their eyes from it. They walked up the road a little way, crossed, and came back to Sienna's car. Sienna knew she would have to come back to take care of all the details, but this morning she was not going to bother Abby with that. She had given their Derbyshire address to the police and hospital, and now thought of nothing else but getting home.

When they were in the car Abby said, 'Did you pick up the money Sienna?' and Sienna nodded as she turned the ignition key. They had brought nothing away except Abby's overnight bag. Nothing at the gloomy flat pertained to their lives now, and both girls felt this keenly as Sienna negotiated the early-morning traffic and headed for the M1.

She drove mechanically, trying not to think of the events of the previous day.

She felt light-headed and knew that some of the shock of witnessing Nick's death still had an effect on her. Abby nodded off in the passenger seat as soon as they were on the motorway, but lifted her head after a few minutes.

'I just thought of something Dad used to say, Sienna.'

'What?'

'He used to say that trouble focuses the mind wonderfully. I never knew what it meant so he explained it by saying that when everything goes wrong and your life is all messed up, you see very clearly exactly what it is you really want out of life. He was right wasn't he? Everything's gone wrong for me and all I can think about is getting home and being home with my sister and my dog and the things I know. Dad was clever wasn't he?'

'Yes,' said Sienna. 'Very clever.' And suddenly, amongst all the deceit and the grief and the worry, the lies and the heartbreak, she thought of Leo. Separate. Inviolate.

Untouched by the chaos that Nick had brought into their lives. Dependable, honest, and worthy of any woman's heart should she choose to give it.

'Abby, get on the phone and ring Leo and tell him we'll be at the farm in a few hours. Tell him I'll explain everything when we get there. And tell him . . . tell him . . . tell him . . . '

'Oh I think he already knows THAT,' said Abby, fishing in her bag for her phone.

When Sienna's Mini came to a stop outside the farmhouse Leo was standing on the porch. Sienna realised that the current trouble had indeed focused her mind wonderfully and she knew exactly what she wanted from life. She got out of the car, walked over to Leo, and buried her face in the front of his sweater.

'Hey,' he said, trying to hold her away from him and see her face. 'What's this then?'

Sienna looked up into Nick's green

eyes but there was no way she was letting go of him. 'I've been to London to get Abby. She discovered she was pregnant and went there with Nick. I took some money for them to help them get started.'

As calmly as she could, Sienna told Leo about Nick's greed over money and how it had contributed to his death. Towards the end she lowered her voice so that Abby would not hear as she got out of the car.

'You've had a bit of a rough time, haven't you?' Leo asked gently. 'Let's not discuss it now. We'll talk later. Let's get you and Abby inside and we'll sort out what needs to be done.'

He took the overnight bag and ushered both girls into the farmhouse. He shushed Sienna when she tried to talk, settled her and Abby into armchairs in the lounge.

Patch came bounding in and gave them his normal welcome. As the day had started off grey and chilly the housekeeper had lit a small fire in the grate and it crackled cheerfully. It was wonderful to be home and Sienna felt warm and drowsy and totally relaxed. Abby went off in search of the housekeeper, to see if she could manage to rustle up some breakfast for them, and Leo came and sat on the floor at Sienna's knees.

'I understand how you must be feeling, Sienna. But I promise you that we will get through this OK.'

It was the 'we' that did it. The calm assumption that Sienna was not alone in this very troubled time went right to her heart and she said in a rush, 'Oh Leo, thank goodness you're here. I don't think I could have born to have come back otherwise. Everything is such a mess. I keep thinking that if I'd shouted sooner to warn Nick about the car, or run towards him, he might still be alive. I can't help thinking that it was my fault. Oh I don't know what to do.'

'Shhhhhh.' Leo got up, picked Sienna up, and sat down again with her on his knee. Her head fell very naturally on to his shoulder and he held it there with his free hand, stroking her hair. 'None of this is your fault. You're a kind, caring person who tries so hard to do the right thing. What happened was dreadful but no part of it can be blamed on you, so stop thinking like that. You've done the right thing. You've brought Abby home. Let's take it from there shall we?'

'All right. I feel as if I should be doing something but I can't think what.'

Leo smiled. 'Here's what's going to happen. You and Abby are going to have a nice lazy day and have something to eat. I'm going to stay here today and be here if either of you need anything. Later, we'll have a talk about handling things in London. I'll drive us down when the time comes and we'll do what needs to be done about Nick. We'll involve Abby only where they want next of kin.'

'That's today, Leo. What's going to happen in the future? About Abby and the baby and everything?'

'Oh I was just getting to that. You and I are going to look after Abby. She won't want for anything because you and I will be there, always, making sure that everything is OK.'

'But how Leo? You've got the pottery and — your own life.'

'Yes, well that's the good bit. You see, you and I will be married and living together — here, or anywhere else you fancy — so we'll be around all the time to make sure things go right. Do you like the plan so far?'

'Married?'

'Oh yes. No doubt about it. Can't have things happening any other way.'

'And Abby and the baby living with us?'

'Of course. Where else?'

Sienna was quiet for a moment, then she said, 'You seem to have this very well planned, Leo.'

'Sorry. But you see, it all got out of hand the moment I met you in the barnyard and you were so cross and you looked so beautiful.'

'There's so much to be done, Leo. Abby's got to get over Nick's death, and we've all got to get used to the idea of the baby and, excuse me, did you say married?'

'Oh yes. Any time. No rush. Will you?' And then he bent his head and kissed her on the lips. It had an undercurrent of passion that made her breathe a little faster and look deeply into Leo's green eyes.

'That was a 'yes',' she said happily.

15

Sometimes, when Sienna looked at what she had done to the small barn in the two years since she'd married Leo, she wondered if her father would approve. The old stone building had been sympathetically renovated and looked very much from the outside as it always had done. The planners had been firm about that.

Inside it was different. The small house had a wonderfully airy feel to it, and Sienna's heart sang each time she visited. Today she had a plate of warm scones which she had just taken out of the oven. She balanced this on one hand while she knocked on the door with the other, opened it and went in.

Abby was in the kitchen, scraping carrots. She had put on weight, her hair was longer, and there was a sparkle in her eyes that had not been there two years before. She was a very natural mother, enjoying every single moment of looking after her daughter. She had discovered the one thing in life at which she was absolutely brilliant, and she was very proud of her sparkling new home and immaculately-kept baby.

Fifteen-month-old Nichola sat in her high chair and held out her arms when she saw Sienna. She had Nick's floppy brown hair and dark brown eyes, but Abby's calm, contented personality. Sienna went over and picked her up.

'You're a very heavy baby,' she said reprovingly. 'We must feed you less. Here, have a piece of scone.' She fed a few crumbs of scone into the child's mouth and then put her down on the floor to play. 'That smells nice Abby. What is it?'

'It's a hot pot. Mrs McKenna showed me her recipe. I thought I might try and make one for Dennis. He's staying for dinner tonight.'

Sienna smiled inwardly but said nothing. Leo's right-hand man at the pottery was a stocky, blue-eyed, straightforward young man with only four passions in his life. The first was Abby, whom he adored. The second was Nichola whom he adored as much as Abby. The third was pottery. The fourth was sheepdogs.

He and Abby were in perfect accord and totally in tune with each other's personalities. There was no doubt in Sienna's mind that this time Abby had found someone who loved her for herself and nothing else. The knowledge warmed her heart whenever she thought of it, and she found memories of Nick and his scheming, slipshod treatment of her sister, fading quietly into obscurity where they belonged. Since Leo had moved the pottery to the farm and into the big barn, Dennis was around a lot.

Nichola had squirmed her way over to Patch's mat, and gone to sleep curled up against him. The other dog, a young sheepdog puppy bought for Abby's birthday by Leo and Sienna, moved over grudgingly and settled down again.

'She thinks she's a dog,' Abby said, laughing.

Sienna was on her way out of the door. 'See you later, Sis. Let me know how the hotpot goes down.' She went out and stood for a moment, listening. Through the kitchen window she heard Abby's off-key humming as she followed her recipe. It was a happy, contented sound and it brought tears to Sienna's eyes.

Farther down the barnyard she could hear shouted instructions from the pottery as someone stacked boxes. An elderly couple pulled up in a small car, got out, and wandered into the gift shop and gallery that had been housed in the middle barn.

As she stood in the barnyard, enjoying the sights and sounds of her new life, Leo walked around the corner, saw her, and came over to where she was.

'I was just coming home to see you,' he said, kissing her. 'I missed you suddenly.'

'What? After being married to me for nearly two years?'

Leo came close and looked down into Sienna's eyes. 'Every minute of every day,' he said gently. 'And hopefully for the rest of my life. Whenever you are near I feel stronger, better, happier.'

'I know exactly what you mean. I've felt that way since the first time I tapped you on the shoulder that day. As a matter of fact we were standing right here!'

They both smiled. It seemed so long ago. Many happy days had obscured the awful memories, and their life together stretched ahead, like a sunlit road. Hand in hand they wandered back to the farmhouse and a future bright with promise.

Other titles in the
Linford Romance Library:

NEVER LET ME GO

Toni Anders

It was love at first sight for Nurse Chloe Perle and ambitious Dr. Adam Raven, but their employer had plans for his daughter, Susannah, and the young doctor. When Adam informed Chloe his career would always come before romantic entanglements, she left the practice for a position far away in the Cotswolds. There, she attracted the attention of Benedict, a handsome young artist. Afraid that he had lost Chloe forever, Adam begged her friend, Betty, the only person who knew her whereabouts, to help him.